D0323448

Manuscript for Murder

Manuscript for Murder

P. J. Coyne

Dodd, Mead & Company
New York

Published by Dodd, Mead & Company, Inc.
71 Fifth Avenue, New York, NY 10003
Manufactured in the United States of America
First Edition

1 2 3 4 5 6 7 8 9 10

Library of Congress Cataloging-in-Publication Data

Coyne, P. J.
Manuscript for murder.

I. Title.
PS3563.A82M36 1987 813'.54 87-15725
ISBN 0-396-09110-5

To the Ladies

Manuscript for Murder

one

When Hardy West entered the restaurant, he paused just inside the door as if to announce his celebrity, but only one person in the Padua Flora recognized him.

From his table along the left wall, Ned Spearbroke watched his friend's entrance and noticed wryly what he had come to call over the years "the Hardy West ID phenomenon."

West looked like a celebrity. Every feature of his face was familiar, the thick, well-groomed hair, the heavy brows, the straight nose, the tapered chin; each taken separately teased recognition but complete acquaintance could never be assembled. Spearbroke thought the gods had been particularly mischievous the day that they had conferred all the appearance of fame on Hardy West while denying him any of its luck.

Such was the case this day as West nodded affably to the maître d' who, though he had never seen West before, very nearly came to attention as the man strode past him toward Spearbroke's table. The restaurant's owner threaded his way through the luncheon crowd, smiling in answer to West's acknowledging smile, to pull out a chair where Spearbroke stood to greet his friend.

"Hardy, it's good to see you," and turning to the restaurant's owner, "Raymonde, Mr. West will have a

Punt é Mes on the rocks with a twist." The owner bowed and nodded as if to thank Spearbroke for supplying the name.

"Yes, of course," he replied. "So good to have you with us again, Mr. West."

"Sorry to be late," West said. "Is this a new place for you?" He took his seat across from Spearbroke and unselfconsciously smiled at two women at a nearby table. They had smiled first, as if recognizing his importance.

"It's my northern Italian season." Spearbroke's brown eyes glinted. He looked at his friend with affectionate appreciation. Both men were in their early fifties, but West's thick hair showed only a few dashes of silver, while Spearbroke's brush cut was quite gray. West's youthful image was supported by luminous eyes, blue pupils set high in pristine white. His tanned complexion and ruddy cheeks gave him a rugged outdoor look and his smile contributed a warmth to his air of mystery and anonymity.

There was no mystery about Ned Spearbroke, for several people in the restaurant, editors and publishers, had had dealings with him and others recognized him from his several appearances on television. His success as a literary agent together with his manner as a man had made him a personality as much in demand on talk shows as were some of the authors he represented. One of those authors was Hardy West, and the relationship between the two men went back more than twenty-five years when both were on the old *Herald Tribune,* working their way through the ranks: West to the politics and government side of the city desk and Spearbroke, eventually, to the book review. When the paper folded, their friendship also took a break, lengthened by Hardy West's marriage to Senator D. A. Prescott's daughter and the couple's subsequent move to the suburbs. The friendship revived a few years later when Spearbroke, in his new role as literary agent, marketed West's first novel. Well reviewed—"an auspicious beginning," the *Times* called it—there had been nothing more for Hardy West except for a few short stories published in literary quarterlies. Again and again, Spearbroke had tried to sell his friend's later novels, and though the prose would always be admired and all the ingredients for good fiction acknowledged, the rejections usually complained about the lack of unity or that the whole manuscript was somehow not as interesting as its parts. West seemed to accept the turn-downs with equanimity, continuing to submit an occasional manuscript to the agent, but as time passed so did his involvement with writing and it had been several years since Spearbroke had read new work from his friend. Their relationship had continued through weekends at West's home in Chappaqua and their occasional meals together in town, such as this one arranged by Spearbroke's secretary after a telephone call from West two days before.

"Whom do we lunch upon today?" West asked ironically.

"Oh, a small paperback sale. Avery's spy story," the agent replied, smiling guardedly. He was never sure if West were upset by his other clients' successes. He never seemed to mind. "How's Libby?"

"Just fine." West smiled at his wife's name. "She's housemothering about two dozen of Cynthia's chums down from school."

"My God," Spearbroke observed as he broke a bread stick in two, "that baby's in college." He looked around the crowded restaurant and at the dapper men and stylish young women. Most of the women sported large, gogglelike sunglasses pushed up at different angles into their hair so they resembled, Spearbroke thought, a bevy of old-time aviatrixes who had just flown in from Floyd Bennett Field. In a year or two, he would look up and probably see Hardy West's daughter among them.

"Here's Raymonde, let's order," the agent gestured toward the owner.

"Listen, Raymonde, how about the truffles?"

"Very good, very good, Mr. Spearbroke," the man replied.

"Truffles?" West inquired, tasting his aperitif.

"A specialty here," his friend told him. "In Italy they use dogs, Dobermans usually, rather than pigs to locate them."

"Cleaner?" West laughed, and looked up at Raymonde.

"Perhaps," the owner said agreeably. "Also the dogs do not like the taste of truffles so they do not eat them as the pigs in France do. Many more are saved."

"Naturally, this saving is passed along to us," Spearbroke said dryly. "Raymonde slices them razor thin into a very light sauce with pasta. You'll like it. Melon first?"

"No, I'll have clams oreganato," West replied.

"And a bottle of something white," the agent said. "You choose for us, Raymonde."

"Thank you, Mr. Spearbroke." The owner bowed, replied, and left.

'Well, now," Spearbroke said. He had fitted a Gauloise into an ebony holder and lit it with a small gold lighter. "What brings you into town? I hope it's a new manuscript. I haven't read anything good in a year."

"You don't sound like you enjoy your work," Hardy West said as he sipped the spicy aperitif.

"I'm immensely fond of its rewards," Spearbroke replied. The cigarette holder between his teeth stabbed the air. "But I don't have to tell you of the crap I go through. It's never been as bad. Thesis writers, thesis editors. Everything written, published to promote a prescribed attitude, almost a party line. Well—" he broke off. He had not intended to give his friend the talk he reserved for unsuccessful clients, but it was almost automatic.

"See that you got a nice offer for Gloria Muller's new book." The writer's tone indicated neither envy nor scorn.

"Yes," Spearbroke replied. "Well, she's really a bloody machine—in more ways than writing. You know." He leaned forward, pausing as a waiter served the melon and clams. The wine was uncorked, tested, and approved. "Here's to your good book." He raised his glass toward West.

"What about Muller?" West said, biting a clam.

"Well, she's apparently set up a private whorehouse just for herself and one or two femme pals. So all that Hollywood loot hasn't gone into just Picassos and Henry Moores."

"All male?"

"Right." Spearbroke nodded, laughing.

"Sounds like one of her novels." West also laughed. A young woman, who had been staring at him from an adjoining table, smiled.

"Old pal," the agent scooped his melon, "I expect to read all about it next year, just before I sell it for a million bucks." They ate then without talking, until West touched his mouth with his napkin and leaned away from the table. He surveyed his friend and agent with genuine fondness, a light in his eye, and took a deep breath.

"Ned, do you remember Adam McKendrick?"

Spearbroke, melon spoon suspended, drew a blank, shook his head.

"The checkers champion of the White Horse Tavern?" West refreshed his friend's memory.

Spearbroke began to chortle. "Of course. Also the scab waiter of the legendary Mother Hubbard strike!" People had turned to look at them.

"Right!" West replied, and snapped his fingers.

"Holy mackerel, that is a name out of the past," Spearbroke conjured. "Adam McKendrick. Well, what's up with him?"

"I got a call from him the other night. He's offered me a job."

"A writing job?"

"Yes."

"Go on," Spearbroke urged, forking his salad.

"Well, it sounds peculiar. Which is why I wanted to talk to you. Apparently, McKendrick has been around city politics . . . I know, I've never heard of him, either. It sounds like flunky, gofer jobs. Anyway, he's apparently collected enough dirt along with the paper cups that he thinks he's got enough for a book. An exposé."

"Oh, dear." Spearbroke raised his eyes wearily. At that moment Raymonde wheeled a small cart to their table and served the entrée. "*Buon appetito,*" he said, and left.

"The thing is this," Hardy West continued. "He apparently was already working with someone else . . . with Dexter Corey."

"Dexter Corey." The agent repeated the name, laughing.

"Right. *As Told to Dexter Corey* from astronauts to hookers."

"Why come to you, Hardy? You're too good for that sort of thing. As your agent, I recommend you turn him down." But upon looking at his friend, Spearbroke saw that his advice was too late. "I see. You've already agreed."

"Not exactly. There's nothing on paper, but," West took a forkful of the pasta, "it's just that McKendrick sent me some of the tapes he had made for Corey and after having played them, I'm afraid it's academic as to whether or not I do the book." The man's voice had become low, almost breathless.

"What do you mean?" the agent said, caught on the other's tense manner. "Isn't Dexter Corey still in the picture?"

"Ned, from what McKendrick has told me, I have the feeling that Dexter Corey is no longer among the living. I'm pretty sure he's been killed."

People at the tables near them were startled by the sounds of Spearbroke choking, his face masked by the white napkin.

"You don't know, then?" the agent said after several deep breaths. "You don't know?" He sipped some water, then some wine, and leaned across the table toward his puzzled companion. "There's no such person as Dexter Corey. Never was. He's a creation of the people over at Stratton to do the as-told-to market. A scissors job done by the anonymous junior editor on call. What did McKendrick say about him?"

"Nothing," West replied, drinking the last of his wine. "Come to think of it, he did say he'd never met Corey. He did it all by mail, sent in his manuscript and they sent back suggestions." West's handsome face had colored and he seemed embarrassed.

"They never talked on the phone about it?"

"Well, yes, that, too, I guess. I don't know." The

writer's manner had become distracted, impatient.

"And a contract? He has a contract?"

"So McKendrick says."

"Sounds strange. God, what a dull story it must be—an exposé of the Lindsay administration. There's been so much of that sort of thing; this manuscript must be a bare-assed wonder." Unconsciously, Spearbroke had peeked at his wristwatch. He had several calls from the Coast coming in at three and it was nearly half past two. His companion became very alert, the whites around the blue pupils seemed to glow in the subdued light of the restaurant.

"It's more than that," he said. "It's sensational—the contracts, the deals, the outright fraud—it's—"and he stopped short, his hands out, as if the enormity of the crimes could not be described, had made him inarticulate.

Spearbroke had reached across the table to take one of his friend's hands, to calm him down. "What is this all about, Hardy?"

"I can't tell you. I don't dare tell you. For your own safety. It's too late for me, I'm afraid."

"Oh, c'mon, Hardy," Spearbroke joked uneasily. "There hasn't been anything dangerous in publishing since *The Secret Diaries of Anne Boleyn*." But West was not to be distracted.

"Whoever Dexter Corey was," he said, speaking almost into the small vase of orange chrysanthemums between them, "then I fear for his life. I am also marked because I've heard the tapes. Ned, McKendrick has tapes!" His voice was low but forceful. "Don't you understand—tapes!" Then his large, handsome face broke open and he laughed sardonically. "You better get to work on making me famous . . . posthumously."

two

The patrons of the Flora Padua saw only the superficial mechanism of the two men's leavetaking, nudged one another to note Spearbroke's slender black cane with its virtuous band of sterling silver. They were unaware of the anxiousness that had caused the friends to forgo dessert, nor even finish their espresso, an anxiety that propelled them out of the restaurant with only a casual farewell to its patron. Spearbroke's unknown companion, it was observed, walked rather hurriedly, head lowered as if against a sudden cloudburst, and it was surmised at a few of the tables that the agent had given the ax to a bothersome and unsuccessful client. Too bad, some of the women remarked, because he had been an interesting-looking man.

Spearbroke returned to his office with an unhappy stomach. He had been eager to see Hardy West, and now he resumed the day's chores with a sourness nurtured by genuine concern for his friend. It was hard to believe that West's life could be in danger simply because he had accidentally heard some old City Hall secrets. So what bothered the agent more was the state of Hardy West's mind. Spearbroke had seen fine talents and sensitive natures broken up more than once upon the treacherous, hard shore of the publishing business. After years of neglect and rejection, perhaps Hardy West had become another casualty.

The offices of Spearbroke, Inc., were on the top floor of a brownstone on East Thirty-sixth Street, near Lexington Avenue. It was where he had started the agency, renting the top floor apartment as a combined home and office, but as one success came upon another, he eventually bought the entire building. He kept the office on the top floor but converted the middle two floors into a duplex apartment and rented the basement to a Chinese restaurant. The terms of the Golden Dragon's lease gave Spearbroke approval of every chef hired by the restaurant. It currently featured Szechuan cuisine, because of a promise he had made himself long ago.

Sitting in a cold-water-flat kitchen, raising cockroaches and eating the instant macaroni dishes he could afford on his copyboy's salary, the young Ned Spearbroke had sworn that if he ever made it, he would eat all of his meals in a restaurant. And if he really became successful, so went the oath, he would own or somehow control the restaurant.

Though the renovations had been extensive, including the small, self-service elevator, he had left the rooms at the top of the brownstone intact; even the old apartment's bathroom with its gigantic porcelain tub was still in the offices of Spearbroke, Inc. Tradition pleased him and there was a Dickensian quality to the main office room, enhanced by the two leather sofas that flanked a fireplace, two gateleg tables with their brass ships' lamps. An Aubusson rug complemented the worn parquet floor, and bookcases went around the walls. Manuscripts, both bound and loose, were piled everywhere—on top of bookcases, in the corners of the sofa, on the tables, even on the floor—and a small gallery of the firm's most famous clients hung impressively on the wall near the elevator. Another reason Spearbroke had not changed the original layout of these old rooms, or moved to the glass cages along Park or Fifth avenues as others had, was because Mrs. Graham would be out of place and uncomfortable anywhere else.

Mrs. Graham was the gray-haired, chain-smoking grandmother of an Olympic track star, and had worked for Spearbroke from the beginning, as receptionist, secretary, auxiliary reader, and morning coffee brewer. After nearly twenty years of association, their relationship was still formal.

"Mrs. Graham," he said, stepping off the private elevator that opened directly into the offices, "would you be kind enough to get those California numbers I lined up, please?"

"CMA has already called back once, Mr. Spearbroke," she replied, an edge in her slight voice. He had taken too long for lunch, it was clear. A cigarette in her hand holding the phone, she methodically tapped out buttons on the panel.

The agent walked down the small hallway off the main room, passed the bathroom, and paused at the closed door across from his office. He could hear his associate's harsh Brooklyn accent in a telephone debate with a publisher. Greenburg specialized in children's books, historical romances, and the two or three authoritative sex manuals Spearbroke permitted them to represent.

He nudged open the door. His petite associate sat with one foot cocked up on the desk, her skirt riding up to her hip while the other foot hooked over the edge of a lower drawer. Flexing the muscles of a leg and thigh, the whole length of limb impeccably put together, she gave a dazzling smile at her employer, the dark eyes large behind heavy glasses, and waved a pencil-fingered hand.

"I'm sorry, Arnold," she droned into the mouthpiece, "I'm sorry to fuck up your digestion, but we are simply not standing still any longer for the usual fifty-fifty screwing on paperback rights." She nodded acknowledgment at Spearbroke as he mouthed a request for her to come to his office. "All right, you take it up with your board and call us back. No sweat," she continued, as Spearbroke crossed into his own office.

Barbara Greenburg had come to him summa cum laude from Hunter College several years ago, originally as a summer replacement for Mrs. Graham, so that the older woman could watch her grandson win the gold medal in the hammer throw. The young woman stayed on after showing a unique gift for marketing juvenile literature and a canny way with publishers. Editors seemed so fascinated by the brassy attack of this diminutive creature that they often found themselves granting terms in contracts that were more generous than intended. In the course of time, their shock turned to respect, even affection, for to the honesty always associated with the Spearbroke agency, she had brought a sense of fun and color. Obscenities and all, she was known as a bright character and this was an asset to the agency.

Initially Spearbroke had been a little put off by her graphic language, as he had also been disturbed by the way she discussed her sexual experiences, freely and in detail. At first, he had imagined that Monday morning recaps of her weekend diversions were intended to tease him from his determination to keep their business and personal lives separate. But she had no such scheme, he finally determined, for she spoke of her promiscuity with the same equanimity as she spoke of her parents in Sheepshead Bay and, in fact, her expertise in the field made her very useful. Two of the firm's most successful properties were the illustrated sexual manuals, authored by a pleasant husband and wife team from Nebraska, and Barbara Greenburg had been able to evaluate the manuscripts with a precise authority.

"It's bullshit and you know it," he remembered her saying to the authors one afternoon. They had put up some defense, features coloring. "Don't jive me," his associate countered. "I tried that position over the weekend and it can't be done." Finally they admitted that the position was more cerebral than corporal.

Mrs. Graham had put through one of his calls to the Coast by the time he reached his desk. He flipped the cane into a brass stand, eased his long frame into the old leather chair before the rolltop desk, took a deep breath, and prepared himself for his role as hard bargainer.

"Hello there, George," he addressed the motion picture producer in California. But the whole time he spoke on behalf of a client who wished to do the film adaptation of his own novel, most of his mind still hovered over the obscure nature of Hardy West's troubles.

In the course of a second phone call, Greenburg clattered into his office on high heels, and continued on through the large French doors to the tiled roof terrace. Spearbroke's mind was further distracted by the picture of his associate watering the banks of plants that made a verdant bower of this corner in midtown Manhattan. Her size and build, together with the awesome sophistication he knew to be stored in that small head, made a very erotic combination.

"What do you think, Ned?" the voice in his ear asked. "Ned?" it asked once more as the agent watched Greenburg ply the sprinkling can over the geraniums. "Ned, what do you think?"

"Well," he cleared his throat, "I think if they are going to offer it, we should accept. This is, after all, your first try at screenwriting although you bring to it all the estimable gifts you have demonstrated as a novelist of the first rank . . ." His voice ambled blindly around the house of praise he had constructed for his successful clients, pausing at all the furniture. Greenburg had finished with the plants and clip-clopped back into his office, her sensuous face serious and preoccupied. Spearbroke mollified his author and hung up. The two agents observed each other.

He fitted a cigarette into his holder, lit it, and leaned back in the chair. She had settled into the old leather sofa by the door, finely articulated knees primly together, composed and attendant.

"Well, what?" she inquired after a moment.

"What?" he asked.

"You asked me to come in here," she said, shifting slightly.

"Oh, yes," he remembered. "Find out who is doing Dexter Corey over at Stratton these days, will you?"

"That's easy. It's a stud just down from Yale. Roger Wallace."

"I take it your knowledge of the young bulldog is more than the usual editor-agent relationship."

The young woman shrugged and looked disdainfully at her fingernails. They were long and crimson colored. "He's just another of those WASP types."

"Don't you know any nice Jewish boys?" Spearbroke asked lightly. It was a familiar subject for them.

"I can't make it with Jewish guys." She laughed and shook her head. "My shrink says balling all those WASPs is my way of saving myself for the right Mr. Yid."

"Back to Roger Wallace. If you're still on good terms, call him for me. I want to talk to him. And Barbara, do you know an Adam McKendrick?"

"Not by name." Her large mouth twisted to one

side. She had sat up attentively on the edge of the sofa.

"I want to go over a few things with you. It looks like we'll get the deal we want from Avon on the Friendly reprint. They'll give us a final answer in a couple of days. Also, the new illustrations for the children's series will be ready by the end of the week. Doubleday is waiting for them, so make sure they—"

"Wait a minute." Spearbroke held up his hand. "Where are you going? These are your projects."

"It's my vacation, dear friend," she reminded him. "It's my annual week leave, starting tomorrow. See the date—April twenty-third."

"Ah, yes," he replied. He wondered what lascivious retreat would frame her revels. One year, her adventure on a ten-day cruise to Bermuda had required a week-long narrative. "All right, leave me notes on where we stand on all that and I'll handle it. Meantime, get me Corey."

Mrs. Graham peered around the doorjamb, patently ignoring the younger woman. "There's a call for you on two-three from a Mr. McKendrick."

"Adam McKendrick?" he exclaimed. "No kidding!" Spearbroke punched the appropriate button on his desk phone and picked up the instrument. "Adam?"

"Hello, Ned. It's been a long time," a husky voice replied.

"I guess it's no coincidence, after all these years, that you should call me. You must know that I just had lunch with Hardy West."

"Well, not exactly . . . but I thought he might call you or something. . . ." The hoarse voice was unfamiliar to Spearbroke, but then he had never really known McKendrick in the old Village days. He remembered him vaguely as a fat, red-faced young man with a gift for puzzles and word games and a superior contempt for those who did not care for such diversions.

"Adam, what in hell is this business that you've got Hardy mixed up in? He seemed really frightened today. Even suggested something . . . well, as if his life were at stake."

"What did he tell you?"

"Not much—political scandal—tapes."

"Tapes?" the thick voice asked. "He mentioned tapes?"

"Yes. What's it all about?"

"I can't tell you right now," the breathy voice replied. "I'm . . . I'm . . ." the voice drifted away as if the speaker were looking about before continuing ". . . on to something that is potentially pretty damaging to a lot of people. Way high up. Anyway, I'd like to get together with you and go over some details as to how to handle it—as long as Hardy has brought you in to it."

"You mean my percentage," Spearbroke said with veiled sarcasm.

"Yeah, sure . . . I don't know where Hardy is staying. We ought to get together this evening. Do you know where he hangs out?"

"I'll try to find him. What's your number?" Spearbroke was mildly angry; he had more important things to do.

"You can't call me. I gave up my phone. I'm in a pay phone on the corner." A heavy truck roared hollowly in Spearbroke's ear. "Locate him and let's meet . . . say around midnight."

"Let's see . . ." the agent paused to check his appointment book. "Okay, where?"

"Do you know Bradley's on University Place?" The voice sounded out of breath.

"Of course. I haven't been down there in years," Spearbroke said, a warmth of reminiscence overpowering his impatience. "It's incredible hearing from you, Adam. Hardy and I were talking about you winning all the checker tournaments down at the White Horse Tavern."

"Yeah?" The man laughed, uncertainly, as if now ashamed of this old triumph.

"What was the name of the owner of the White Horse? He always said he wanted to be buried under the floor of the barroom. I wonder if he was. What was his name?" Spearbroke asked.

"Wasn't it something like Andy? Andy, wasn't it?"

"Yes, Andy. All right, I'll try to locate Hardy and I'll meet you at Bradley's at midnight."

"What's all this about?" Barbara Greenburg asked. She had listened to the last of his conversation from the doorway. "A reunion of the old Village crowd?"

Ned Spearbroke told her the story, including Hardy West. But when he told her of West's thought that the ghost for Dexter Corey might no longer be alive, she snorted. "You have proof to the contrary," he said.

"Sure," she said, and shrugged. "You can't talk to him right now because he's on an extended vacation in Canada."

"Why extended?"

"Well, I talked to a gal I know over there. He had ten days coming and went up to Nova Scotia. Then he wired for another week and that's been used up. In fact, she says, they may can him. No great loss," the young woman said in a tone that Spearbroke felt judged more than the fellow's editorial gifts.

"Barbara, you've never cared much for Hardy West—the man or his work?" The woman was now perched on the edge of the sofa, her face serious.

"I've never met him, except by phone. But as to his

work, there's something . . ." She paused, her face elevated as if she hoped to scent the word in the air.

"What . . . tell me?" Spearbroke had learned to appreciate her judgments.

"Well . . . *impotent* is the word, I guess." She smiled with apology. "It's just an emptiness in the middle of all those pretty words. Like some of the creeps I meet. They sound great until they're brought up to it. I don't know." She crossed her legs. She wore no bra and the pert shadows of her breasts shifted beneath the cashmere sweater. "It might be me," she continued soberly. "It may be just my lower-middle-class Jewish background, but Hardy West marrying into the Prescott family like that—well, it somehow might have jinxed him as a writer, as a man. I don't know. Who was it called the Prescotts 'the sick Kennedys'?"

"I can't remember," Spearbroke said.

His associate continued. "Old Senator Prescott didn't do much for the constituency at Sheepshead Bay. And then there was Libby and her brother running around defacing synagogues . . ."

"They were only children when that happened . . ."

"So they were children," Greenburg shrugged. "Is it true," she asked with a smile, "that the Prescotts put up twenty-two of the original bucks that bought this island from the Indians, and that they're still collecting the interest?" She paused and looked down her nose. "Then there's Libby."

"Libby? What's with Libby?" Spearbroke idly swung his chair from side to side.

"If only she weren't so goody-goody." The young woman grimaced. "I'd feel differently maybe, if it weren't for the fact that all the middle-aged men who try to pick me up seem to be married to women like Libby Prescott."

"To change the subject," the agent said, "where are you going on vacation?"

"To Yoga camp."

"Yoga camp?"

"Sure, they run a camp in one of those old mansions out on Long Island."

"Sounds celibate."

"Well, maybe I'm getting older . . ." She got up to leave, then turned back. "Anyway, I picked up this kinky bastard in Soho over the weekend, and some of the things he got me into will last a long time. Want to see my bruises?" Her hands had gone to the edge of the sweater, to pull it over her head, but Spearbroke turned away blushing and she giggled with a stagey throatiness.

The remainder of the afternoon passed quickly. Spearbroke gave only half his attention to the details of the business while the rest thought about Hardy West.

Greenburg had poked into an area where he had made some speculations as well. Spearbroke knew many instances of a painter or writer marrying into wealth and being no worse off for it. On the other hand, some creative temperaments could respond only to adversity, could develop only in a plain, if not impoverished, environment. Hardy West might be one of those talents, for as one rejection after another met West's manuscripts, Spearbroke had begun to wonder if his own support had been based more on sentiment than genuine critical evaluation. Greenburg had used the word *impotent*. He could understand why. Each of West's new works seemed to become more attenuated, more abstract, dreamlike; perhaps the easy existence afforded Hardy West by his wife's income may have smoothed away the grit necessary to ignite a talent. On the other hand, could he have been wrong about the value of that gift in the first place? It was never easy to tell about creative talent, and their friendship made it even more difficult.

"Boss, I'm leaving." Barbara Greenburg addressed him from the French windows. Spearbroke, as was his custom in fine weather, was reading manuscripts on the terrace, sitting in the shade of a large green awning that pulled down from the west wall of the building. She came and sat beside him, the fragrance of her perfume (Madame Rochas) rather heavy for her fragile person, though suited to the dark hair and eyes. "How's the new Hobson?" she asked, fingering the manuscript in his lap.

"She's angrier than ever," he replied. Spearbroke placed his hand affectionately on the smooth surface of her bare knee. "Have a good time," he said sincerely. "Get some R & R and remember, we'll miss you." She had been watching him closely, almost as if in a daze, and then something flashed in her eyes, a glint like the sudden turn of a fish in a bowl. She leaned forward and kissed him on the cheek.

"I bet you're a dirty bastard in bed," she said with a wicked smile.

"Come now, Greenburg, control yourself." He laughed, with another pat on the trim thigh next to him. "You'll spoil your attitude for Yoga camp. Have a good time. Now go," he said, giving her a gentle push.

The young woman walked to the French doors, her high heels echoing on the tiles of the terrace, and disappeared into his office. Ned Spearbroke was suddenly aware of a longing, a sense of desire. He stared at the empty doorway, then got up to follow her, but at the entrance to the office he heard the hum of the self-service elevator as it carried her down to the street.

three

Long after Mrs. Graham had also made her humming descent to the street, Spearbroke moved off the darkening terrace and down to his duplex apartment and into the bedroom-library, a balcony running the width of the building that was suspended above the brownstone's second story, a space only incidentally used for sleep. Floor-to-ceiling bookcases made up its three walls, cases so high that a caster-wheeled ladder was required to browse their top shelves. There were no windows at this elevation. One section of the bookcase swung open for entrance to a large dressing room and bath.

The area's illumination was subdued and cozy, marked off, it would seem, into various reading areas. Brass-fluted *Belle Époque* light fixtures bore twin green glass blossoms at regular intervals around the bookcases. The back wall was built around a three-quarter-size antique bed said to have been transported by Napoleon to Moscow, and a carved walnut screen that once separated ladies from the hurly-burly of the medieval scene masked the flying edge of the cantilevered floor. Through the interstices of carved vines, the immense room below could be viewed. Its most important feature was a large Oriental rug that overflowed the floor and curved up one bare brick wall to be suspended near the ceiling on a heavy brass rod like a red and blue waterfall frozen by a spell cast in an Arabian fairy tale.

By nine o'clock he had finished with the Hobson manuscript and was partway through a batch of essays by another client, but he put them aside, wearied by the temper of the collection. He fit a cigarette into its holder, stood, stretched, and walked over to lean against a bookcase. His thoughts kept returning to Hardy West. He moved to a large leather chair only to get up when his stomach reminded him he was hungry. It was three hours before he was supposed to meet Adam McKendrick at Bradley's so he had plenty of time for supper at Irene's. He changed to slacks, turtleneck sweater, and slipped into some loafers. Just as he slung on a tweed jacket, a peculiar noise turned him toward the front of the building.

It was his private elevator, but like all familiar sounds heard out of context, its whining hum at this hour sounded an eerie note. The machinery had clicked on, the dynamo whirred. Sometimes Mrs. Graham returned after office hours to type up a contract. Perhaps Greenburg had forgot something.

He peered through the medieval convent screen. The illuminated cab of the elevator was just passing behind the frosted glass door at his apartment level and continued to the office floor above. The machinery clicked off. Then as if the passenger had had a change of mind, the machinery clicked on again, the whine recommenced, and the elevator passed his apartment level once more, going down. It reached the ground level and clicked off. Silence. Spearbroke listened for footsteps, for the elevator door to slide open. There was no noise. Nor did he hear the outside door close.

Quickly, he went down the spiral metal stair that connected the two floors of the duplex and pulled out a heavy black thorn cane from the rack in the foyer. He pushed the button by the art-deco-paned door of the elevator. Again, the machinery set in motion, the panel illuminated as the elevator rose. It stopped. Spearbroke gripped the cane and abruptly pulled open the door. The cab was empty.

He stepped in and pushed the button for the top floor. The elevator rose and halted opposite the entrance to the agency's office. The door was still locked, there were no marks to indicate tampering, but he unlocked the door anyway and stepped into the darkened room. He looked everywhere—even the bathroom. Nothing was out of order.

On the way down to the ground floor, he noted the small business card of a manuscript typing service stuck into the edge of the control panel. There was nothing else in the elevator. Mr. Li of the Golden Dragon had seen nothing, no strangers entering or leaving the building; however, it was a busy night at the restaurant. Spearbroke looked east, then west down the darkened street, puzzled but not alarmed. Perhaps a vagrant or a prankster.

Lexington Avenue was quiet, almost deserted as that part of town usually is at night. Only the heavy, guttural exhaust of a bus down a few blocks disturbed the peace. Uptown, the series of traffic lights were clicking from red to green in sequence. There was no one on the sidewalks. Spearbroke strolled east, swinging the heavy cane, and flagged a cab on Third Avenue for the trip uptown. There had been scratches around the lock of the outside door, but how recent they were he did not know. He had never really looked closely at it before. On the jolting ride he reviewed who had keys. Mrs. Graham. Greenburg. Mr. Li at the restaurant. One or two old girlfriends had keys, but they would have called in advance.

Irene's was filled with the usual Friday night

crowd, a mixture of chic suburbanites who had read about the place in *Time* or *Harper's Bazaar* and the celebrities who, with no other place to go on a Friday night, permitted themselves to be observed as they ate the soul food that Irene provided. Spearbroke preferred the place on Tuesday nights, for pals who worked at *Sports Illustrated* usually came there then, since that magazine's deadline made Tuesday part of their "weekend." He walked past the bar where the tourists stood four deep, to the round table that the large black patroness kept available in the front for her special friends and backers.

The table was empty, though the stained cloth indicated that some so favored had already dined there. Irene came toward him with that rolling gait that always made Spearbroke think of a gently rocking bowling alley. The black moon of her face was eclipsed by her welcoming smile.

"Hello there, baby," she crooned. "You just missed Mailer."

"How was he?"

"One order of chicken, two of greens, and an apple cobbler." Irene put one hand behind her head and snapped her fingers. A waiter appeared swiftly and changed the linen on the table. "Are you eating or drinkin'?"

"Honey, I'm starving."

"That's fine," she smiled. Her voice was feathery. "We got knuckles tonight and the ribs are real good. Also chitlins." She made a wry face.

"What's the matter?" he asked.

"I'm going to take them off the menu come Monday. We don't sell chitlins worth a damn. All you white liberal types are always talking 'bout 'em but none of you ever eats 'em." She swayed like a happy circus tent.

"I'll take the ribs, sweets, yellow rice, and a side order of peas. And a tequila sour on the rocks, no fruit."

"Check," said Irene and turned away, then revolved back again with her remarkable grace. "Oh, yeah. Someone was in here earlier looking for you."

"Who?"

"I don't know him." The tone of her voice suggested an attitude toward this unknown; someone who had dared to come into her place and ask for one of her regulars. "Had a funny name."

"What did he look like?"

"On the pretty side, but straight. His name was a direction. Like South."

"West . . . Hardy West?"

"Yeah. Who's he?" Irene asked suspiciously, rearranging one of the bentwood chairs.

"He's a client, a friend."

"A writer? Never heard of him," she said, and left to give his order personally to the cook.

Ned Spearbroke was amused by the woman's reaction to Hardy West. He was unknown to her. He had intruded into her domain. It was a unique place of recognition she had carved out of the indifferent rock of Manhattan—with a little help from people like himself—and she jealously guarded the privacy that the restaurant provided her special customers. True, Irene made her money, a good deal of money, from the gawkers who ate or drank while they ogled the famous at the next table, but she would not tolerate anything more than covert glances. Staring was out and her nephew, a young man of linebacker proportions, enforced the rule. Not bad for a girl from Central Park North, Spearbroke mused as the tequila warmed and relaxed his stomach.

Spearbroke's thoughts shifted to the permanent

niche in anonymity apparently destined for Hardy West. The episode at the restaurant earlier that day, the writer's effect on that room full of people, was in strange contrast to his abrupt dismissal by the overnight worldliness of Irene. And the fact that West had been looking for him reminded the agent that Mrs. Graham had been unable to locate the novelist. Where had he been? Spearbroke would have to meet McKendrick alone, and he was already bored by the prospect. Now, West was trying to locate him. Perhaps, if he stayed at Irene's long enough, the writer would show up again.

Lifting a second tequila sour, the agent pondered the up-and-down movements of his unknown caller this evening, another sort of mobility closer to home. A burglar, he puzzled, would prefer to come over the rooftop or even use the narrow auxiliary staircase at the rear of the building; not take a leisurely ride up and down in the elevator. He made a mental note to have all the locks changed in case this had been a scouting expedition by some second-story thief. Then he sat back and relaxed.

Mildred Bailey sang "Gypsy in my Soul" (Irene personally selected the records for the jukebox), the spareribs had been "real good," and the ambience of the place worked a gentle conspiracy on Spearbroke. Moreover, as usual, there were extraordinarily interesting-looking women to observe. Spearbroke exchanged a few words with several, but for the one sitting with a large party in the rear, he reserved a smile of recognition.

They had been lovers and adversaries before and during the presidential race of 1968. She still resembled those spaniellike young women who had worked for Gene McCarthy or Senator Goodell. Advertising agencies had appropriated the loose-jointed, long-boned image of these elegant women to sell their products or was it, Spearbroke often wondered, the other way around—had this breed of young women taken their image or style from commercials for cigarettes and deodorants?

Nancy Morrison's success as a talk show hostess, then television commentator, indicated that her similarity to these other women was superficial; a biological chance that had enclosed a hard, aggressive intelligence within a soft, beautiful envelope. The neat connections of that delicate body were still savored by Spearbroke in memory. As he sipped the after-dinner Wild Turkey sent over by Irene, the agent watched from the corner of his eye. The tall blonde stood and walked to the front of the restaurant. She moved with a half smile and one hand partly held out as if to ward off, in the kindest way, any suburban tourist who might be so tactless as to ask for her autograph in these "off duty" surroundings. The large gray eyes, further enlarged by contact lenses, looked at everyone and no one with that impartial myopia that afflicts the famous in public places.

"Hi," she said. He noted she still wore Aliage.

"Hi," he nodded. "Can you sit?"

She took the chair next to him, winding long legs around each other. The camel hair pants suit complemented her tawny complexion. "What's new?" she inquired.

"Well, someone tried to break into my place tonight." He told her of the incident with the empty elevator. "Then I have a client who thinks he's going to be murdered because of a ghostwriting job he's accepted."

"Wow," she laughed. "I didn't think anyone took books that seriously anymore. Bring him on the show, why don't you. Who is it?" As she spoke, she had taken possession of his gold cigarette case, opened it with a familiar ease, and extracted one of the Gauloises. He held the lighter as she leaned forward.

"Oh, he's a novelist, a friend." He remembered her pose, that slant of hair falling forward, the line of eye and mouth pursed around the cigarette as, in the middle of a night, the flame had illuminated her face. "His name is Hardy West."

"Hardy West," she exclaimed softly, blowing up the smoke and leaning back in the chair. A small gold pocket watch hung in the deep valley of her bosom. "He was just here a little while ago. That's funny, too, because I've never known him to hang out here."

"He was looking for me, I think," the agent replied, then looking at her closely, said, "I didn't know you knew Hardy West."

"Oh, just for a little while." She shrugged. "A while back."

"How while back?" Spearbroke said, moving his leg away from the pointed toe of her boot.

She spoke as if challenged. "You seem surprised that I would know him."

"No, not really. It's just that . . ." He paused while she gave a negative shake to the inquiring waiter. ". . . it's just I've never heard any gossip about him. He didn't seem like the type who would stray."

"What type is that?" she asked, her large eyes growing larger with feigned blankness. "*Everyone's* that type." She looked around the room. "As for Hardy West . . . I could make you out a list right here."

"Well," Spearbroke replied, very surprised and a little chagrined; only a few moments before he had been feeling sorry for his friend. "How did you meet?"

"Must have been a party. I can't remember. It didn't last long. In fact, we only . . . oh, two . . . three, maybe four at the most," she counted on long slender fingers.

"Maybe five or seven," the agent suggested. She smiled and snubbed out the cigarette. "What happened?"

"He was funny." She leaned forward. "Very domestic. That was the problem—his problem. He was always doing things."

"Doing things?"

"Yes, building things, fixing things. You know, like he was the building super. One time I came home from the studio and he had all these plumber tools that he had bought and he was fixing my shower. That was what really finished it."

"Why was that?"

"Well, it was my shower. It was my drip, you know?"

"Yes, I remember," Spearbroke said. Their eyes met.

"Who fixes your breakfast these days?"

"Mrs. Graham brings a thermos of coffee and a couple of rolls."

"You better watch out. Those older women can kill you." They both laughed but then she was very solemn with a sudden shift of expression. "I still make coffee that way you showed me—with cinnamon."

"Now, Nancy," he cautioned her.

"Ned." She leaned toward him, a hand on his knee. No one in the restaurant gave them any attention. The young woman removed her hand, but her face remained close to his.

"What about you and Schneider? I read somewhere you and he were making it legal."

"He's down in Augusta for the Masters," she answered.

"He's got thirty pounds on me," the literary agent told her. "He could put me halfway down the fairway."

"I need to talk to someone," she said a bit raggedly. "Forget them," she tossed over her shoulder when he had looked back at the table of people she had deserted. "They're only network types. Ned," she implored. He raised his hand for the check.

* * * * *

Their lovemaking was as exuberant and as adventurous as it had been during their affair years before, but something was lacking, some element of passion that might have lifted it above the category of a complicated, if not prolonged, handshake. Nor did the problem she had been so desperate to discuss with him turn out to be anything more urgent than her habitual self-flagellation on the subject of her son, a teenager who was working his way through the different disciplines of psychoanalysis. He had heard it all before and, in fact, it was the tedium of these sad sessions postcoitus that had broken his attraction to her because it was all she could talk about or wanted to talk about.

Nancy Morrison lay across his lap, cornsilk hair splayed over his belly as she murmured her agony into his groin, the occasional cold pellet of a tear punctuating his flesh. He made out the details of the room in the dim light. Abstract drawings, rococo furniture, books and periodicals stacked on the thick pile rugs, and in one corner glinted the steel shafts of golf clubs, apparently the property of her current lover, the PGA champion. Idly, the agent amused himself with images of Schneider taking a few practice swings with a driver before hopping into bed or later studiously working with the putter as Nancy narrated the tearful history of her motherhood.

He ran together the events that had brought him against the silky padding of this headboard, and the picture assumed the likeness of Barbara Greenburg. Her image on the terrace this afternoon seemed to flood the darkened bedroom. Unexpectedly, Greenburg had set off desire within him, not just her self-advertised availability, but something about her, her jaunty arrogance and good humor, and he had satisfied that desire meretriciously with the first surrogate that had come to hand. The aftertaste of bourbon made him swallow several times. Unconsciously, he had moved his position in the bed, as if to get away, but the naked confessor in his lap snuggled closer. He longed for a cigarette, but his case was out of reach.

"My God, what time is it?" He sat up suddenly.

Interrupting her litany, Nancy Morrison pulled herself over his body and leaned nakedly over the edge of the bed to fish among the clothes and jewelry on the floor.

"It's almost two, it's Saturday." She pulled herself back onto the bed and sat cross-legged. "We'll have a nice brunch."

"I'm not hungry," he answered, thinking it was a communion he did want to take. "I have to make a phone call."

The bartender at Bradley's answered, and the owner, Bradley Cunningham, was near the phone.

"Adam McKendrick?" Bradley's soft voice replied. Spearbroke could imagine the rugged face of the man as he talked from the end of the bar. "No, he wasn't in. He won't be coming in."

"What do you mean?"

"Seems like he was mugged. I was just reading about it in the early *News*."

"Mugged?"

"Yeah. Found him in the foyer of his apartment.

Stabbed . . . let's see . . ." He paused and Spearbroke could hear the cool, vibraphonic sounds of the weekend combo. "It says here," Bradley continued, " '. . . a former minor official with the Lindsay administration was found dead of stab wounds in the lobby of his apartment building, apparently the victim of a mugging assault. Police give robbery as a motive, as McKendrick's watch and wallet were missing.' . . . You knew him?"

"A long time ago," Spearbroke said thoughtfully. "Any time given about the murder?"

"Naw," Bradley replied. "The body was discovered a little after seven last evening. Hey, there was someone in here looking for you tonight."

"Hardy West?"

"A lady."

"What time was that?"

"Around midnight, I guess."

Spearbroke hung up, puzzled.

He was unraveling the tangle of their clothes as Nancy Morrison returned to the bedroom, nude and bearing two glasses of bourbon and ice. She groaned softly as she saw him pulling on his pants.

"Don't go," she said gently.

"I'm sorry, Nancy, but I must. Something crazy . . . well, I don't know what to make of it . . . but I—well, Hardy West really might be in danger. I've got to try to find him."

"Please stay," she cajoled. Her lips squirted the ice cube she had been sucking into one drink. She leaned over and fastened her mouth to his left nipple and gently bit him. "I'll do something special for you," she offered.

"I can't." There was nothing special anymore that

anyone could do, he thought, and the woman assumed her caress caused him to shiver.

* * * * *

The regular ticking of the cab's meter sounded unnaturally loud on the deserted, silent street before his brownstone. Only the working lights in the kitchen of the Golden Dragon faintly illuminated the sidewalk. He had paid the driver and turned toward the building as the car pulled away when he was pushed to his knees from behind.

A thick arm went around his neck, a knee was pressed between his shoulder blades. Spearbroke tried to move, gasped, kicked about him ineffectually.

"What? . . . What?" he choked. His assailant muttered something into his ear, pushed him onto the sandstone steps, and ran away without another word, leaving him breathless, angry, and frightened. However, his mind edited the husky sounds made into his ear until they became intelligible. "Stay away . . . West!"

four

The next morning Spearbroke placed a person-to-person call to West at his home in Chappaqua. He had had a few hours of exhausted sleep and had treated the abrasions on his knees and hands with peroxide after a long hot shower. No, a young woman told the operator, her father was in New York City for the weekend. Was there a number where he could be reached? Just before Spearbroke had collapsed into the Bonaparte campaign cot, he had checked the apartment and the office above. Nothing had been disturbed. Perhaps the Princeton Club, Hardy West's daughter suggested.

But the Princeton Club knew nothing, nor did any of the other places Spearbroke knew Hardy West sometimes frequented. The Landmark Tavern on Eleventh Avenue. The Chelsea Hotel. The Cookery in the Village. A bar called Stryker on the West Side. Spearbroke left messages in every place, thinking it was strange that he knew places where his friend sometimes ate, drank, and slept, but knew nothing of his personal life, as Nancy Morrison had revealed. Well, West had apparently known Adam McKendrick. Now Adam was dead.

The Golden Dragon closed on the weekends and Spearbroke was suddenly very hungry. He pulled on a pair of slacks, a shirt, a corduroy jacket, and an old pair of sneakers. It was one of those hard, bright days that polish the city in early spring until it gleams like the cheap kitchenware for sale in Fourteenth Street bazaars. He strolled down Lexington Avenue and then across to Madison Square where he bought the *Times* and, finding a pushcart, bought two sausage and onions on seed rolls, washing them down with a bottle of orange soda.

"Stay away . . . West." The warning had become familiar in his memory now, for he had turned it over and over so many times since last night, trying to discover what it was about the words, the voice, the tone—even the crushing grip around his neck—that registered somewhere. The gratuitousness of the warning was almost comical, for it seemed impossible to get close to West, let alone to stay away from him. Had he ever been close to him? People like Nancy Morrison and Adam McKendrick had known him better, it would appear.

He would have to find Hardy West in order to take the warning seriously; though, as he sat down on a bench, his bruised knees reminded him that his unknown assailant had been serious. Pigeons swirled around the statue of Admiral Dewey to begin a migration to the south end of the park and the statue of William Henry Seward. The chimes of Metropolitan Life tolled the hour. If it were not for such bells, Spearbroke reflected, would any of the people in this area, including himself, know their position in space? Pigeons, he had read, had a sense of space, an inner compass that referred to the sun's angle in the sky, but human beings required artificial means to establish their position.

Without touching any of the familiar points of his compass, Hardy West had become lost to him. Temporarily out of contact. Adam McKendrick had been located. The pointed blade of an urban thug had permanently fixed his place in time and space. There was no abstraction about him. He had been summed up forever—a former minor official in the Lindsay administration, the newspaper had termed him. Whatever hopes or ideals McKendrick may have had in the old days when they used to drink at the White Horse had been used up in the turnstiles of existence: token dreams.

That phone call from the dead man bothered him. There had been something about it which had perplexed Spearbroke but which he could not separate from the rest of the vague picture he had of McKendrick. He squinted up into the brilliance of the sun above the Flatiron building; it was something the man had said, but he could not identify it. He conjured up once more a picture of McKendrick, an image some twenty-five years old and faded, but still a few details clear. The man's obesity, considered jolly when young, must have become awkward, even offensive with age. His rankling sense of superiority. Hadn't McKendrick majored in physics? Spearbroke seemed to remember him telling jokes with punch lines that involved electrons and quantum graduates. No, in none of the jumble of his memory could he find a clue to what had disturbed him, still nagged him about the dead man's call.

According to the address Spearbroke read in the *Times,* McKendrick lived within walking distance of the park where he sat in the sun. He was tempted to stroll west across Twenty-third Street toward the location, but he knew what it would be like: a tenement in the Chelsea area, the air rich with dog feces and other decomposition. The paper said there had been no survivors. So much for Adam McKendrick, fat, florid-faced, checkers champion at the old White Horse and a former minor official with the Lindsay administration. Spearbroke stood up, walked from the park, and dropped the newspaper in a trash basket, then stopped. But a minor official who had secret tapes and was about to expose them.

His answering service passed along only a few items: several calls from a man who would not leave his name or number, one call from Libby West who would call back later. In the early days of their marriage, Spearbroke had spent a couple of weekends at the Wests', and as he returned Libby's call he imagined the old house on the Prescott estate that Hardy West had made over. There had been something very touching about the way West had taken hammer and saw to the building's interior, as if his self-taught skill as a carpenter were something he brought to their marriage, like a dowry, for Libby Prescott could have hired a team of the best craftsmen to do over Stanford White's original design for the estate's old gatehouse. Spearbroke let the number continue to ring, though it was obvious no one would answer, for he enjoyed the picture in his memory of Hardy West fitting paneling, measuring and cutting fresh lumber for shelves and cabinets. It all seemed so much easier in those days, a simple matter of making the correct measurement and cutting along the lines. Everything had fit together, or seemed to.

That night he dreamed Adam McKendrick called him and they talked about the old days. The man's voice kept fading away and coming back so that what he said made no sense. He hung up on him and then the phone chimed again, but he refused to answer it. It continued to sound until finally he was awakened. The phone really was ringing and it was Sunday morning.

"Oh, Ned, I hope I didn't wake you," Libby West said in his ear.

"You did, but it is time I was up," he replied. "How's Hardy?"

"I don't know. I thought you would know. I haven't heard from him since he came into town to see you. I'm rather worried." Her voice snagged on half a laugh.

"Maybe he's off for Tahiti," Spearbroke suggested, immediately sorry for the poor jest.

"I really am worried about him, Ned. I looked for him all last night. I've looked for him in all the usual places."

"Oh, was it you at Bradley's?"

"Hardy sometimes meets people there. I thought he might show up. Ned," she paused, and in his mind's eye he visualized her face tighten with anxiety, ". . . may I come see you?" The fruity consonants and flat vowels of the upper-class Eastern seaboard accent seemed strained.

"Of course. You mean now?" Spearbroke looked about the library. The Sunday edition of the *Times* he had picked up Saturday night was scattered all over the floor.

"Yes," Libby West replied. "I'm in town at one of Pa's old digs."

"Fine. Give me a few minutes. You know, I have no kitchen here and can't offer you anything."

"Yes, I know—I'll bring breakfast," she said quickly, and hung up before he could say good-bye.

He had showered and dressed and reread the *Times*'s review of a client's new book before the downstairs buzzer signaled. He waited by the elevator, but the cab passed by, continuing on to the office floor.

"Oh, damn," he heard her say, "I pushed the wrong button. I'll be right back." Then, from above, "There." And the mechanism clicked, hummed, and the elevator returned. It stopped. He opened the door for her.

She had brought some packaged doughnuts and

coffee in an antique stainless steel thermos that reminded Spearbroke of old grads tailgating at the Harvard-Yale game. She also had a bundle of large yellow tulips.

"I couldn't resist them," she told him. Then, looking about his apartment, "You do have water here and perhaps an empty bottle of some sort?"

Spearbroke rummaged about in the small pantry bar at the rear of the living room and found a pitcher. After putting water in it, he returned. Libby West was standing by the large divan in the center of the room, her back to him as she unwrapped the flowers. Morning sunlight through the front windows bleached out the colors of the tulips and her pale blond hair. Her slim figure was X-rayed through the linen shirtwaist dress; she seemed to be wearing very little underneath. Her sandaled feet were high arched and delicately boned.

"There," she said, arranging the flowes in the vase he had given her. They divided up doughnuts and coffee.

"You mustn't be worried," he said finally. "He's working on a new book and . . ."

"I know all about that," she said quickly. "Some nonsense about an exposé of the Lindsay administration. Who would care about that?" She tilted up her head. She had crossed her legs and leaned forward to hug herself. She drank none of the coffee nor touched the pastry. Nor would she, he was fairly sure. She observed her foot gently swinging back and forth as if it timed her thoughts. Her expression was preoccupied, early risen and freshly accomplished. Indeed, there was an athletic grace about her that was rather sensual. "It's his own work I'm worried about," she continued soberly.

"Well, this won't hurt him," he advised her. "It often has a good effect to do something completely different."

"But this?" She looked up to startle him by the intense blueness of her eyes. "This dreadful business, meeting hack politicians in bars." Her long, thin nose sniffed something bad.

"Come now, Libby." Spearbroke felt almost fatherly, though she was only a few years younger than he. "You grew up in that atmosphere; it didn't do you any harm."

"Precisely," she replied, sitting up. The word had been pronounced with a faint sibilance, a slight whistling through the well-cared-for teeth. She smiled. "None of that bothered me because I'm tough." She continued swinging her foot. "Really tough, Ned." She repeated the adjective with her small chin thrust out as if in proof. "But Hardy is a creative person. Oh, I know, he's big and strong and very . . . but inside, inside," she tapped her front, "he's fragile. You must know that."

"Did he tell you anything about his book? About McKendrick? He told me some story the other day about being afraid for his life, because of information he's learned."

"Oh, that." She dismissed her husband's fears with a wave of the hand. Gold chains rattled on her wrist. "Yes, he told me all that." She observed the agent. Spearbroke began to feel awkward under her stare and turned around to locate some cigarettes.

"Can we be friends, Ned? I mean real friends," the woman implored, touching his hand.

"Of course."

"Oh, I know we've known each other for some time, but that's not really the same thing. I want you to be my friend . . . I really need someone, someone to . . ." She had abruptly turned away from him and looked up at the carpet sweeping down from the wall. The skin was taut over the high cheekbones and her eyes glistened. "I'm afraid, awfully afraid that Hardy . . . has become . . . unstable."

"Oh?"

"Well, first there's his work. You know all about that. I don't have to tell you." She rushed through a prepared list. "Every artist needs some acceptance . . . someone to say, 'Yes, we like this piece. We'll take it.' That hasn't happened, as you well know. And he writes beautifully, doesn't he. Doesn't he? Yes. But after a while he has to have someone besides me . . . and you." She looked him directly in the face, blue eyes appealing. ". . . someone beyond that select circle to accept him."

"Well, Hardy has grit, Libby. He can stick it. He's very serious about his work."

"If it were only that," she sighed. The large chair enveloped her as she fell back, arms up and hands over her face. "I don't have to hide from you our situation . . . the financial, I mean. It seemed to be an idyllic arrangement for years . . . I had all the money, and, well . . . I'm indifferent to money." Her smile was apologetic. "And Hardy could write, could create without worrying about—"

"Now listen," Spearbroke said, putting out the cigarette. "You're getting yourself into a mire. I hate to sound like an agent but the market for fiction today, particularly the kind Hardy does, is lousy. The editors are all humanoids programmed to accept one-dimensional, tacky confessionals. Hardy knows all this; he's a pro, and he accepts it. Your paying the bills has never bothered him. Come on, Libby. After how many years of marriage, you're not suddenly thinking that Hardy married you for the Prescott fortune?" For a moment, he was tempted to tell her of the warning given him—

"Stay away, West"—but just as quickly decided it would only upset her more.

"No, I don't," she replied evenly, sucking part of her lower lip between her teeth. Her hands were now in her lap and she seemed childlike. "I don't . . . but how about him? I mean, maybe he's begun to think so. If he just had a little success, something to make him feel . . . well, less dependent . . . Have you read any of his new novel?"

"New novel? I didn't know he had a new novel. That's splendid."

"He's been working on it for about a year now," she said dully.

"Have you seen it?"

"Some of it. It's quite beautiful."

"Oh?" He watched her as she slowly stood up, now looking weary, the freshness that had accompanied the cut flowers, wilted. She moved around the chair; leaned against it, her back to him.

"And there's something else," she said with a distance in her voice. "Hardy has become impotent." She took a breath. "He hasn't made love . . . been able to make love . . . for a long time."

"What?"

"We've tried." She turned around, a wry smile beneath the china-blue eyes. "He can't get it up, as they say." The broad "a" of her accent gave the expression a perverse inflection. It would have been funny under other circumstances. "So you see." She gestured and the gold chains rattled.

"My dear Libby."

"That's why I'm afraid for him." She spoke in a rush now. "All of these burdens . . . these silly burdens on his manhood . . . and then this . . . the final proof, well, it may have just driven him over . . . he's out there and I don't know where and I must find him . . .

I must . . ." All her composure disappeared. She ground one small fist into the palm of the other hand.

Spearbroke jumped up and put his arm around her, held her as she shook, vibrated like a struck tuning fork. The muscles across her shoulders and down her upper arms were hard and tense. She looked up at him. The eyes were unnaturally bright, and with no recognition. "He's all right, Libby. We'll find him. Don't worry. I'll put out some more calls around town."

"Yes. Of course. Yes," she said, revolving slowly within his loose embrace. "Silly of me. I'm sorry, Ned." He admired the way she forced composure back into a deliberate poise. "I hate scenes. I must go." She turned away and picked up her small purse from the chair. "Call me if you locate him. I'll do the same. Thank you." She had extended her hand like a good sport. Her eyes were again bright and intense. Her grip was firm and straightforward. "We really are friends, aren't we?"

Spearbroke took her hand.

"I want to be friends with you," she said, coming closer. Her eyes had softened, shadowed by lowered lids. Her lips pressed together then slowly parted just as she kissed him. "Friends," she murmured. It became more than a friendly kiss very quickly. "Oh, my God," she breathed and ground against him.

"Libby." Spearbroke was burned by the intensity in her frantic body. He held her close as she had begun to shake again, the vibration setting off ripples along his own thighs.

"My God," she moaned. Her fingers worked frantically at the buttons of her dress, then the garment slipped off her shoulders and down her body. She had been wearing nothing underneath and her slender nakedness pressed against him. "Oh, Ned," she said feverishly. "You kept looking at me with those eyes and I nearly . . . came twice."

The rest of that afternoon, Spearbroke reviewed the depth of his friendship with Hardy West as he made love to the man's wife. He and Libby seemed to have fallen into a Lawrencian parody, sweaty and sharp-toothed, that assaulted the furniture, seized the floor, and railed against the ottoman. At one point they had fallen apart, and she had noted the abrasions on his knees and he then told her of being attacked two nights before and of the warning. His bruises moved Libby to kneel before him and kiss them tenderly, but her healing attentions evolved into caresses that incited another frenzied bout of lovemaking.

Prolonged orgasms withered the patrician plainness of her features; the nose thinned and the arc of forehead had become shell-like. They rarely kissed. But this slim woman generated more erotic power than most of the women he had known, and he guessed it had something to do with her money, for to tumble the Prescott fortune in one's arms was to satisfy two lusts simultaneously. He wondered if a man might make too many trips into that rich vault.

"Let's put this in perspective," Libby West said during another pause. She had crawled to the Plexiglas table and lifted a cup of cold coffee. Her hand trembled, and the heavy nipples of her small breasts released the tremor. "I'm not just a horny lady on the verge of middle age. At least I don't think I am." She smiled but looked above his head. "Nor does this have anything to do with Hardy."

"Of course not," Spearbroke said, only to answer. His knees burned. "Don't worry," he soothed her, though he wasn't sure what he meant. "These things happen. It's better to have them out, get rid of them."

She nodded abstractly and observed the reflection

of her fingernails as they tapped the top of the coffee table. "That's true, though it's never happened to me before." She smiled slightly. "Would it be farfetched to think of this as an act of friendship. Can this still be a real friendship?"

"Sure," he finally said.

The friendship was celebrated again and they took the elevator to the top floor. There was something so perverse about going barefoot and half clothed around the literary agency, she with her dress hanging open, that he was aroused instantly upon getting off the elevator. He lifted her upon the long table in the reception room and took her quickly. The brief, explosive act was audienced by his clients on the wall, including the broad, handsome face of Hardy West.

It seemed that once she had explored his body, Libby West now desired to nuzzle all the things that occupied him at his work. She picked up and read sections of manuscripts, asked questions about an author she liked and another she had only heard about. She discovered Greenburg's office and Spearbroke found himself telling her all about his associate, including the young woman's bizarre promiscuity, while Libby listened with a distance in the blue eyes. He began to feel peculiar talking about Greenburg this way, revealing confidences about her to Libby, almost as if he were a man telling a strange woman, a pick-up, about his wife and going into such detail, accounting such secrets that are possible to reveal only to strangers.

Late in the afternoon, they had separated, she sitting in Greenburg's office to read, and he in his own office, as if their new intimacy no longer required closeness. He wondered how Mrs. Graham would react if she suddenly poked her gray head around the door to find him at his desk, wearing only a short robe, looking over a manuscript biography of Lon Chaney. He settled for an image of complete accord, an unshakable equity of expression on the grandmotherly face.

"What is this?" Libby asked. She had come into his office with one of the sex manuals the firm had sold. Her nose wrinkled and the thin upper lip curled slightly as she flipped through the pages and glanced briefly at the photographs that illustrated the book.

"A money-maker," he told her, putting aside his own reading.

"Nasties," she said, dropping the book on his desk. It was the same face she had made earlier when he was describing his associate's peculiar sex habits. "I've been thinking about what's just happened," she told him. "Us." She sat down on the edge of the large leather sofa across the room, her dress partly buttoned. Her knees were together, hands clasped and face alert.

"And?" Spearbroke urged her. He suddenly felt silly, and pulled his robe closed over his nakedness.

"I have to face up to it," she spoke earnestly. "I am getting to be a middle-aged lady, and I haven't had sex in a long time."

"Oh, dear," Spearbroke sighed. "And I thought you said it was something about my eyes."

"Well, it was. It was," she assured him quickly. "No, it was all those things, everything coming together."

"Quite so," he murmured.

"You're impossible," she laughed. "I'm trying to be serious about this . . . my first act of unfaithfulness to Hardy."

"Mine too," Spearbroke observed, and looked out on the terrace. The leaves of the geraniums stirred in a slight breeze. "Incidentally, shouldn't we give another try to find old Hardy?"

He called the Chelsea, the Princeton Club, and a few other places. The answer was the same at all of them; Mr. West had not been around. He kept his hand on the phone after the last call, fingering the buttons on the panel as he regarded her. She was calm and poised, a little wan perhaps, but with strength declared by the small, pointed chin. She returned his look evenly, without the shadow of a blink.

"Perhaps we should notify the police. What do you think?" he asked. "This business with McKendrick."

"Oh, my." She pulled her hair back tight on her head and then released it. "That will make a big thing, won't it? I mean, the family connection and all that. Maybe he's just stashed away somewhere with this silly book."

"I can have some inquiries made that won't get to the press," Spearbroke said. "I know someone who's rather high up in the Department, from the old days on the *Trib*. He knew Hardy in those days, too, as a matter of fact. It could all be handled very discreetly."

"Oh, Ned, I don't . . ." She looked away, and rotated the gold wedding band on her left hand.

"Libby, if Hardy is in some sort of trouble, we ought to try to help. After all, McKendrick's mugging might have been a murder—Hardy did tell me he was in danger."

"Of course, you're perfectly right," she said, standing up. She set her shoulders and fastened the top buttons of her dress. "Yes, all right." Then, as if looking about the room for a clock, "I must dash."

Spearbroke's robe fell open as he stood up and he casually employed part of Lon Chaney's life as an inadequate disguise for his nakedness. It was even more ludicrous on the trip down to his apartment, and he laughed. "Just the picture we make in the elevator," he answered her look. "It's a little reminiscent of a big weekend at the Hotel Dixie." Her eyes, as if just noticing his lack of clothes, had traveled down his body to the groin, and turned back to face the front of the descending cab, as if she were a proper matron determined to ignore the pervert with whom she was temporarily enclosed.

Once the decision to leave had been made, Libby West methodically went about the arrangement for her departure. She used the bathroom and had the stainless steel thermos recapped and tucked under one arm before he had even been able to pull on a pair of slacks. She waited for him patiently in the living room so that he could escort her to the street.

There was a heaviness in the air as if rain might be on the way. He had waved to a taxi several blocks up Lexington Avenue. As they stood on the corner waiting for it to make a light, he noticed that she had fixed a slim gold barrette in her hair, pulling one side up and off her face. They did not speak. But when the taxi pulled over, she turned quickly to him, one hand against his chest, her lips pressing his mouth as perfunctorily as the words they pronounced.

"Ned, I feel bad about this. I feel that I have used you," she told him quickly.

"Oh, that's all right," he replied. "You can cry on my shoulder any time."

"Thanks ever so much," she said almost gaily as she slipped into the taxi. "But it wasn't your shoulder that I needed."

five

Toward noon on Monday, Mrs. Graham's fruity contralto interrupted Spearbroke's review of a contract. Without rising from her desk she announced the caller's name from the reception room. "Inspector Gambino is returning your call."

Spearbroke punched the illuminated button on his phone panel. "Hello there, Lou. Thanks for calling me back."

"How are you, Ned? How have you been?"

"Just fine. How's Camille? The kids?"

"Camille is fine and the kids are no longer kids. Nick is getting his law at Fordham and Marie made us grandparents last fall."

"Well, well."

"What's on your mind?" the police official asked.

"I seem to have a missing author," Spearbroke tried to joke. "You used to know him. Remember Hardy West . . . in the old days on the *Trib*? He was on the police beat for a while when you were at the Eighteenth Precinct."

"Oh, yes. The guy that married Senator Prescott's daughter. Is he writing books now?"

"For some time," Spearbroke replied, vaguely annoyed.

"So, he's missing," the other said after a moment, with some disinterest.

"Well, I don't know . . . it's a little complicated," the agent continued, feeling foolish. "He seemed to be working on something with Adam McKendrick who . . ."

"Uh-huh . . . I read about McKendrick in the papers," Gambino interjected. "He was working with him on a book? What was it—a ghost job?"

"That's right."

"Okay. Go on."

"Well, I had lunch with him several days ago . . ."

"When was that?"

"Ah . . . Friday."

"You had lunch with him three days ago, then."

"Yes, three days." Spearbroke could almost hear the stroke of the pen as Gambino took notes. He had used an old-fashioned Esterbrook fountain pen in the old days. "He was very upset, even talked about being fearful for his life and then with McKendrick being killed, I—"

"Wait a minute." The other stopped him. "Did West say who had threatened him? What was this he was working on, some sort of exposé?"

"No, he mentioned no names, just that he was afraid. He really was afraid, Lou. And it *was* an exposé."

"Of the Lindsay administration?" the police official asked incredulously. His laugh was low and humorless.

"Well, yes," Spearbroke replied, feeling awkward again.

"So West has been missing for three days. Maybe he's got some gash somewhere. These writers are always in the saddle with someone, aren't they?" Inspector Gambino continued soberly. "All right, Ned. I'll put you onto someone at Missing Persons and . . ."

"That won't do," the agent replied, surprised by

the snap in his own voice. "I'm really calling for his wife. She doesn't want this spread all over page six of the *Post*. You know how the Prescott name would attract attention. I'm really concerned, Lou. There are other things as well."

"What things?"

Spearbroke told him about his unknown assailant, the warning he had received, and this information changed the official's attitude. During a long pause, Gambino's voice was muffled by the hand he had placed over his mouthpiece. He carried on a long discussion with someone in his office. There was laughter, more talk, and the voice returned clearly. "Okay, I'll tell you what I'll do. We got an outfit called the Major Case Squad. They work independently and can cut across departments. They're very savvy guys, and they got a lotta contacts. I'll get someone there for you and there won't be any fuss. Okay?"

"I'm much obliged," Spearbroke said.

"Sure. No problem." He rang off.

Ned Spearbroke had lunch on the terrace outside his office, a plate of Zen Schan Szu Pe-ah sent up by the Golden Dragon. He could hear the rustle of paper as Mrs. Graham ate at her desk. She always brought her lunch in a small brown paper bag and thereby had become a legend among the executives and authors who visited the agency during noon hour. On his last trip to the Coast, an important film producer spent most of one evening telling dinner guests about this remarkable woman. People like that made too much of Mrs. Graham's habits, Spearbroke always thought, though he was not unaware or ungrateful for the character she gave the agency.

Nancy Morrison had been taping an interview when he called her, and did not return his call. He tried her again late in the day but she had left the studio. Nor was she home, and the answering service was uncommunicative. He spent the rest of the afternoon composing a letter to an author who had lost whatever spark had attracted Spearbroke in the first place; then he scrapped the three-page draft and opted for a short and more merciful two-paragraph note of rejection. Mrs. Graham stopped her typing to answer the phone, and called out, "Roger Wallace."

"Who is Roger Wallace?" he asked. There was no answer as Mrs. Graham awaited his decision. "All right, I'll take it." He picked up the phone. "Yes?"

"Yes, sir. What can I do for you, sir?" The young man's voice rang with a brassy deference that put Spearbroke on edge.

"Hmmm . . . I called you, didn't I?" he replied, trying to sort out the name.

"While I was on vacation" the reply came back, and something clicked.

"You're Dexter Corey these days?" Spearbroke said, remembering the connection.

"That's right. What can I do for you, sir?"

"We represent Hardy West, and it's my understanding that he's working on a book with you."

"No, sir," the young editor said abruptly. Spearbroke had never taken such an intense dislike to anyone so quickly.

"He's not?"

"No, sir" the reply shot back. Then silence.

"Well, just a minute . . . it was my understanding that he was working with Adam McKendrick on a book for Stratton . . ."

"No, sir" came the voice, this time almost sporting with the negative.

"Would you mind being more specific?" Spearbroke said, making a note to call the president of Stratton, then scratching it out.

"Well, frankly, I wasn't aware of West being involved," the young editor said quickly. "I had only dealt with McKendrick . . . the late Mr. McKendrick, to be specific. But no contract was offered."

"No contract. I see. It was some sort of an exposé, was it?"

"Yeah. Are you ready: of the Lindsay administration?" Mr. Wallace's laugh was as annoying as his speaking voice.

"I take it to mean that the details were not that startling?" The other's silence affirmed his thought. "And the writing?" he asked out of curiosity, "how was the writing?"

"Specifically," the editor paused, "it was shit." Spearbroke was surprised that he had not added *sir*. "An incredibly amateurish mess."

"I see," the agent managed to say softly. "Well, thank you, Mr. Wallace. Perhaps we will talk again in circumstances more beneficial to us both."

"No sweat," the man replied. "Enjoyed it." And he hung up first.

Spearbroke replaced the telephone, ran a hand over his brush cut. "Now what the hell is this all about?" he asked himself.

Just before Mrs. Graham left for the day, he lounged in the leather sofa across from her desk and put his feet up on the large sea chest that served as a table. She had put her desk in order, covered the large electric typewriter, and had washed and freshened her makeup in the bathroom. She now stood rubbing some lotion into her large, well-shaped hands. The office was silent, the phone that seemed to ring continuously all day long had been stilled magically by the hour.

"What do you think is going on with Hardy West?" he asked her.

"He's such a nice young man," Mrs. Graham said

gently. "I hope nothing really bad has happened."

"What do you think? Do you think he's in trouble? Where has he gone?"

Mrs. Graham shook her head. "But I don't think it has anything to do with his book about the Lindsay administration. After all, the newspapers wrote everything there was to write about that. No, I think it's more personal."

"Personal?" Spearbroke studied her broad face. She had surprisingly few wrinkles for a grandmother.

"Well," she smiled at him over her glasses. "Mr. West is a very handsome man and it just may be a personal matter."

"Personal? You mean . . ." and he paused to gauge her expression, then added, "you mean, personal."

"Yes, personal," she said, and snapped her purse and stepped into the elevator. When the hum of the life had ceased and he heard her open and shut the street door, Spearbroke walked about the empty office suite as if looking for something, but did not know what or where to find it. Greenburg's silent office made him melancholy, and that sense of guilt he had experienced when he talked of her with Libby West was reawakened by the items on her desk, the Miró print on the wall. In the reception room, he idly aligned the issues of *Publishers Weekly* and *Bookman* on the table. For a long time he leaned against the doorjamb of his associate's office. Then, shrugging, he sat down at the desk and used her phone to try Nancy Morrison once more.

"Hello." Her voice was fresh and surprised him. She sounded in one of her manic moods; perhaps because her lover had birdied his way into a three-way tie at Augusta on Sunday. "Oh, it's you," she said more evenly.

"You didn't return my call," Spearbroke continued. He pulled out the bottom drawer of the desk and rested his foot on it.

"I'm mad at you, you jerk," she said half seriously. There were succulent noises, liquid and continuous.

"Are you eating something?" he asked.

"Some leftover chicken," she said between bites. "I'm not really hungry, but it satisfies my oral compulsions."

"Indeed," Spearbroke replied. "May one offer congratulations on the events at Augusta yesterday?"

"One may." Her lips smacked. "What's this about?"

"Nancy, I must ask you something . . . personal. But I need to know."

"Yes."

"It's about Hardy West . . . how was he . . . how did he perform?"

The agent had to hold the phone away from his ear until the woman's whoops and whistling subsided. "Ned," she finally said breathlessly. "You're worried," she moaned with exaggerated compassion.

"I have never worried," Spearbroke told her coolly. "This has to do with something else. His work."

"Okay," she paused. "On a scale of one to ten . . . well, I'd put Hardy around eight, a strong seven, maybe. The first time it seemed like a ten, but that was just because it was the first time and then, nobody's a ten. Yeah, I'd rate him a strong seven."

"Really," Spearbroke replied. "And how long ago was this . . . this . . ."

"About six months ago . . . Yes, that's right, it was around Christmas, because one time we exchanged gifts."

"I see," Spearbroke replied, puzzled.

"You sound surprised." Her voice remained cheerful.

"Well, I thought it may have been longer ago, your affair. Say, when you were both younger."

"Don't try to be cheeky—you don't have the build for it. I wasn't the only one. He's a truck."

"I can't believe that."

"Why can't you believe that? You mean you don't want to believe. It's true." She paused, apparently to search for a particular morsel for Spearbroke's benefit. He was treated to the greasy sounds of chewed gristle. "I could tell you names that would surprise you, women he made it with. Hardy is very good with women, I don't mean just the sex. He likes us, he really likes women. He does a lot of little things, thoughtful, nice. Unlike some people I know."

"I like you," Spearbroke protested.

"You think we're amusing, droll, something to pet when you get tired of reading."

"I protest," he said with some seriousness.

"Up your protest," she replied, chewing. "Back to Hardy, you mentioned something about performance before. There was a suggestion now and then in bed that he expected to be graded, you know? Sometimes he seemed under pressure to deliver, and that could turn you off."

"By the way, when did your champion leave for Georgia?"

Spearbroke thought of that heavy arm around his neck and the strength that pushed him into the stone and cement.

"Who, Schneider? Four, five days ago. Why? Oh, c'mon." She had caught his thought. "There's none of that with him; he's a pussy-cat. Anyway, he never knew about me and Hardy. I don't think."

"I'm really getting worried. I've called the cops."

"Ha." Her voice was liquid. "What a waste of the taxpayers' dough. They'll probably find Hardy shacked up with a librarian somewhere, building bookshelves for her."

"Nancy, this is serious."

"You're such a prig. Listen, I'm finished with this chicken leg. Maybe you ought to hang up."

He did.

In Tuesday's mail there was a postcard from Barbara Greenburg. The picture was of a large stone mansion, typical of those built by railroad magnates on the South Shore of Long Island at the turn of the century. On the reverse side, his associate's neat script inscribed a message in green ink.

Boss,

Great time. Some of the positions in the original Sanskrit are very dirty. Should see me in the Plow. Outta sight! Also: Have I got news for you about HW???!! See you soon.

Love,
BG

He had not expected Libby West to answer the phone herself. Her voice was slight, hesitant. He told her of the arrangement with Inspector Gambino and then mentioned that Barbara Greenburg apparently had some information.

"It may only be some sort of gossip," he cautioned her. "Anyway, I thought I'd bring you up to date." He paused and looked across the room to the leather sofa. He could see her sitting on it, pale and drawn. "How are you?" he finally asked.

"Fine," she replied offhandedly. "Why don't you come out here? Can you come up for dinner tomorrow night? Junior would like to talk to you. There's a train at four that will get you here in time for cocktails. And if you wish," she paused and his pulse jumped, for his mind's eye had screened the image of her tongue, pressed against the thin upper lip, ". . . if you wish, you may spend the night."

Spearbroke carefully noted the appointment on his desk calendar and asked Mrs. Graham to check the trains to Chappaqua. His secretary had also received a postcard from Greenburg and, to his surprise, the message was propped up against the bud vase on her desk.

"I see you've heard from our gypsy, too," he said.

"Um-huh," Mrs. Graham answered. She rolled a multicarboned pack of bond into her typewriter. "It was nice of her to send me a card," the older woman said sincerely. Her broad torso swung around on the swivel chair. "The place seems awfully quiet with her gone, I think." She had become self-conscious, blushed, and cleared her throat. "By the way, I managed to get a couple of tickets for the Miller play for Grace Watts."

"Oh, my God." Spearbroke struck his forehead. "I forgot all about her." One of his most successful authors was making her semiannual visit to New York from Chicago. "She's here now, isn't she?" Mrs. Graham nodded, her expression skeptical, amused. "I have a dinner date with her, don't I? Well, let's see. She and her husband stay at the Gotham. Call them. Tell them we'll meet for supper after the theater."

"Where?"

"Yes, where?" Spearbroke said, suddenly unable to think of any place in Manhattan.

"The last time she was here, she said she wanted to go to Irene's," Mrs. Graham reminded him.

"I'm not going to take her to Irene's," the agent said quickly. "I know. Les Pyrenées on Fifty-first

Street. That's near their theater. I'll meet her and her husband there after the show. What a week, what a week," he grumbled as he walked back to his office. "You picked a fine time for your deep-breathing exercises," he cried through the open door at Greenburg's empty office. The phone rang again. "Never mind," he yelled over his shoulder, "I'll get it. That's what I do around here, is talk on the phone. This goddamn phone is going to grow out of my hand one of these days . . . Yes, hello!"

"Mr. Breakspear?" a man's voice asked.

"The name is Spearbroke," the agent snapped.

"This is Detective Ryan at Major Case. I have a note here from Inspector Gambino to contact you in reference to a matter that is pertaining to one of your associates."

"Oh, for Christ's sake," the agent sighed.

"I'm sorry?" the other queried.

"No, I'm sorry, Mr. Ryan . . . Detective Ryan . . ." Spearbroke took a deep breath. "Did Inspector Gambino tell you anything more?"

"The report here has to do with a missing person subject, one Hardy West, with suspicion of foul play due to some unspecified connection with a recent nine-o-two, the victim's name to be Adam McKendrick."

"That's correct," Spearbroke replied. There was no answer and he could hear the click-clacking of typewriters in the background. "Well?" he finally said.

"Yes, sir?" Detective Ryan asked.

"I was hoping," the agent said, "that you could help me locate Mr. West. I am calling on behalf of his wife who was . . ."

"Yes, sir, I am familiar with Mrs. West's background," the detective replied. Spearbroke could not ascertain the man's age, but he sounded young, a boy tenor who had handed in his choir gown. "I have also made some inquiries about Mr. West and I am sorry to say there is nothing to report."

"This won't do," Spearbroke said, suddenly exasperated and angry that he should be caught up in this mess. Damn Hardy West. Damn Greenburg. Damn Libby too! His carefully modulated schedule of work, reflection, and pleasures had been shredded. "Let us get together," he said into the mouthpiece as he flipped through his appointment calendar. "Here. Lunch tomorrow. How's that?" He scratched off a date with an editor.

"Lunch tomorrow?" the other said slowly, as if he were looking at his own appointment book. "I generally don't eat lunch, Mr. Spearbroke."

"Lieutenant Ryan," the agent nearly shouted. He felt as if he were trying to communicate through a soft blanket.

"Excuse me, sir. I am not a lieutenant but a detective, first grade."

"And excuse me, Detective Ryan." Spearbroke chastened by the man's unruffled seriousness. "I apologize for my tone but I am most distressed by my friend and client's disappearance. Can't we meet for lunch and start over again? I'd like to talk to you. There's a restaurant called the Golden Dragon, on East Thirty-sixth Street, near Lexington Avenue."

"Proximate to your place of business, is it not?" Detective Ryan asked.

"It is," Spearbroke replied. "Shall we say, tomorrow at twelve-thirty?"

six

Spearbroke almost wheeled into the Golden Dragon at noon the next day with the enthusiasm of a schoolboy at term's end. Dinner with Grace Watts had not been so bad and he had turned the novelist and her husband over to Mrs. Graham for the day. Being a devoted reader of the woman's fiction, his secretary was happy to act as the Cicerone to guide the visitor through the mysteries at Bloomingdale's. As he fitted a Gauloise into the holder, he began to feel easier, more relaxed than he had since this whole business with Hardy West began, and he knew that this calm was bolstered by the expectation that he was about to hand over the fate of Hardy West to someone else.

The man who followed Mr. Li from the front of the restaurant made the tiny Chinese seem even smaller. But his size was not so surprising as his age, for he looked to be in his sixties, in great contrast to the youngish voice that Spearbroke had heard on the phone.

"Detective Ryan, Mr. Spearbroke." The policeman extended a large, rather soft hand and the agent shook it without rising. The whiskey tenor was the same.

"Delighted to meet you," Spearbroke said, observing the other carefully. The loose flesh on the full face was pink, and the eyes were very blue and sparkled. White hair with a tight wave in it that in another day would have been called marcelled. A deep dimple in the closely shaved and powdered chin. The man looked more like an old-time political hack than a police detective. "I'm just having some sherry. Will you have a drink?"

"I don't think so." Detective Ryan lifted shoulders that seemed to take up the width of the booth, and fetched out from his coat pocket a small black notebook. He licked a thick index finger and pushed the looseleaf pages up and over.

"Well, then, let's order," the agent said, turning to Mr. Li who stood by the table. "I'm rather hungry, Mr. Li, so I shall have the Kung Paw Ha Szning with an order of Szu Scham Tay-dey. Perhaps some Wo-Buja's, small order."

The detective interrupted the review of his notes to barely look at the menu beside his plate. "Just bring me some chop suey," he said. Mr. Li didn't respond, a mask of nothing on his face.

"Perhaps a Number Four will do." Spearbroke suggested one of the combination luncheon plates the restaurant put together for office workers in the area.

"Lissen." Ryan's hand took Mr. Li's coat sleeve to detain him. "I get rice with that? Okay. Bring me some milk, too. Thanks a lot."

Spearbroke sipped his sherry, took a final drag on the cigarette, and pistoned the butt into an ashtray. He looked at the detective. The other began talking without looking up from his notebook.

"This is the busiest time of the year for Missing Persons," Detective Ryan declared, the high voice almost jocular. "Nothing's turned up there on your friend yet, but it may take them longer than usual to give a definitive answer."

"Why are they so busy?"

"The time of the year. The floaters."

"Floaters?"

"Those bodies that have been in the rivers during cold weather. When the weather warms up, so does the water, so they all rise to the surface." There was almost a smile on his face when he faced Spearbroke, but the blue eyes had the clear, cold quality of a trout stream. "They got a lot to do this time of year," he explained.

"I'm sure of it. I am sorry to take up police time with this—"

"Not to worry," Ryan interrupted with a broad grin that deepened the chin dimple. "If it wasn't this one it would be another, and, anyway, I like one of these cases once in a while. By the way, how'd you know Gambino?" While he had been talking easily, his eyes had made a complete inspection of Spearbroke.

"I was a reporter on the old *Trib*," Spearbroke told him. "Lou Gambino was at a nearby stationhouse. We got to know each other that way, also—a few beers now and then. We've kept in touch."

The detective nodded, rubbed a thumb into the crease between his nose and cheek, and looked away with a wry smile. He leaned back in his seat, pressed against it so the lacquered wood creaked. His eyes played an idle tag with the fans and paper lanterns that hung from the ceiling.

"I have discovered a few things that perhaps you should know about," Spearbroke said. The detective leaned forward to lend circumspect attention as the agent told him of his conversations with Nancy Morrison and the young editor at Stratton Publishing. He took no notes.

"So as it turns out, there was to be no book at all," Ryan said smoothly. "As to this young woman's report—By the way, can I have her name?"

"I'm not at liberty to . . ."

"Oh," Ryan agreed. He had not taken out a pen, so

he either expected such an answer or did not care what the answer would be. Perhaps he already knew the name. "Pertaining to your friend," he continued, "my inquiries would indicate that he had no trouble in that department. That he was something of a ladies' man. Also, as to his being a writer, there are no books by him in the library."

"Well, that tells more about the library than it does about Hardy West," Spearbroke said, fixing his napkin as a waiter brought their food. For a moment, his loyalty amazed him.

"This was the New York Public Library," Ryan replied softly. Methodically he mixed up the combination plate set before him and lifted a forkful into his mouth. Spearbroke used chopsticks, deftly turned a slice of fish in the sauce, and tasted it. He rearranged the spiced cabbage and lifted some of that to his mouth. "What books have you sold for him?" Ryan asked, chewing and swallowing.

"Unfortunately only one, but," and the agent stopped, angered by the glint in the other's eyes, "you'll have to take my word for it, Hardy West is a fine writer. It's the nature of the publishing business that . . . What about McKendrick?" He changed the subject.

"The medical examiner is reviewing the case. Victim was discovered in the vestibule of his building." Ryan referred to his notebook. "Multiple knife wounds, upper thorax, hands, and neck. Victim's apartment disorderly. It could have been ransacked or he might have been a slob. Incidentally—" He looked up smiling, freed from the formality of his notes "—he was a crank letter writer. Almost a professional letter writer, you might say. Investigating officers found boxes of letters he had written to the newspapers, mostly the *Village*

Voice. They were all about the social welfare department. He was," he looked back at his notebook, "he was an assistant deputy something or other appointed in the Lindsay administration. And you know, a few samples I've seen of the letters weren't so far wrong, either."

"I see." Spearbroke tried some of the sizzling rice, mixed a piece of fish with it, and tasted more.

"The funny thing," the detective continued, "is that the guy was getting unemployment himself. He also had a sideline. He redid burned-out bulbs for motion picture projectors. He had a workshop in his bedroom. He'd collect burned-out lamps, cut them, redo the filaments some way, then re-fuse the glass and sell them to theater operators for half what they'd pay for new ones. He was an interesting type," Ryan concluded, nodding his head and smiling. He had pushed aside his combination plate, and taking the bowl of white rice, dumped several packets of sugar over it, then poured on the glass of milk and ate the whole thing with a spoon. Spearbroke watched, fascinated. "I got to like it this way when I was in the Army at Fort Bragg," the policeman explained simply.

"Since you haven't mentioned it," the agent returned to his own meal, "I assume no manuscript was located." The detective shook his head as he spooned the rice.

"No. Nothing but carbon copies of all these letters he wrote. I mean, hundreds, maybe even thousands of letters. We got a couple of men looking them over in case there may be something there."

"He made carbon copies of the letters he sent to newspapers?" Spearbroke had a mental picture of the fat McKendrick he knew as a youth, studiously typing long criticisms of the social system, full of scientific jargon and formulae. The detective had nodded and sipped some tea. "But what about the manuscript? The exposé? And there were supposed to be tapes also."

"No tapes. No manuscript." Detective Ryan referred to his notes. "Also, no typewriter. Some of the letters were dated only a couple of days before his death, so he had a typewriter until very recently. This we can be sure of. It may have been stolen by whoever killed him. They can be turned over easily on the street, you know."

"Or whoever killed McKendrick took the typewriter *and* the manuscript, *and* the tapes . . ." Spearbroke let the sentence hang in the air. The detective only nodded and looked sad. "I don't like this one bit," Spearbroke said.

"Now, who did know about this manuscript, this so-called exposé?" Ryan had turned over a page of the notebook.

"Hardy West. The editor at Stratton Publishing. Well—his wife, Libby. And me. There may have been others."

"Was there anything in it that would have to do with Mrs. West's family?" Detective Ryan eyed Spearbroke sternly as the agent guffawed. "Well, I was just thinking because of her father, the Senator, some political angle there might have come out in this McKendrick's research."

"Old D. A. Prescott was out of politics long before Lindsay became mayor. It's true, there were rumors about the old guy making certain deals with the syndicate." Spearbroke paused for verification, but the detective's expression was impassive. "But it was never proved."

"This assailant the other night," Ryan said, "can you give me any more of a description now?"

"No, just that he was big and powerful. Heavy arms."

"Anything about his clothes. How did he smell? His voice?"

"Nothing more than what I've already reported," Spearbroke replied. "It's very confusing."

"How well do you know Mrs. West?" the detective asked; the blue eyes had become buttons.

"Oh, Libby?" Spearbroke swallowed. He wondered if the little black book contained anything about their tryst. "Well, I've been to their home, talked to her on the phone. In fact, I saw her just this last Sunday." Ryan had nodded and gone back to scooping up rice and milk. "She came by to ask me to help her find her husband. What do you make of all this, Detective Ryan?"

"What do I make of all of it?" the man asked, taking a last spoonful from the tilted rice bowl. "So far we got no reason to believe the McKendrick homicide involved nothing more than a simple A-and-R. As for your client—no offense, now, but you asked me my opinion—he's a no-visible-means, and they usually fall into a pattern."

"What's that mean?"

"Of support. No-visible-means-of-support. I have to look at it different from you, Mr. Spearbroke, and I know he's your friend as well as your client. But you just admitted that you haven't sold any of his writing for him. How has he been living all these years? His wife is rich. Right?"

"Yes, all right." Spearbroke put down his chopsticks and wiped his lips with the napkin.

"Now, that's okay. Nothing wrong with that—Women's Lib and all that. You know, some guys are lucky," the high voice acknowledged with no appreciation. "That's all." The heavy shoulders dismissed judgment. "But there may be a couple of patterns overlapping here. First," he flipped a page of his notebook, "subject is fifty-one years of age. That's the age when some men change jobs, women, and locales. Also, a second factor, sometimes these no-visible-means get . . . well, they want to *do* something. When we find them, if we do find them, often as not they're doing something completely different from their past nature, like driving a taxi or slinging hash in a diner."

"I hardly think that will be the case with Hardy West," Spearbroke laughed. The image of his handsome client as a short-order cook was amusing. "He's a writer."

"Well, even writers have to eat." Ryan used his napkin and tucked it beside his plate. "And maybe there's good experiences in driving a cab."

"But you'll keep looking?"

"Oh, sure," Ryan replied, folding up his book. "Gambino has taken me off everything else for a while." A significant, almost mean look nicked Ryan's eye when he said "everything else" as if to challenge Spearbroke to ask what the man's more important cases were, but he did not take the dare. He was sure the answer might have something to do with a suspected plot to blow up the United Nations.

"Okay, Mr. Spearbroke, I'll stay on it," Ryan said, rising like a towering genie from the booth. "If you think of anything let me know."

seven

That afternoon Libby sent the gardener down to meet him at the station in Chappaqua, and the man raced the Mercedes sedan along narrow roads winding through dense woods as if he were eager to return to his hedge clippers. He was silent on the trip to the estate and only when they stopped in front of the Tudor-timbered stone gate house did he speak to Spearbroke, directing him to the tennis courts, taking his overnight bag into the house for him.

Tack-Top, Tack-Top, Tack-Top, Tack-Top . . . Top. The sound of play guided Spearbroke along the graveled path. *Swack-Top . . . Tack-Top . . . Top-Top . . .* He was in a corridor of confined and excessively groomed Lombardy poplars that intersected a smooth wall of impenetrable privet. The path took a sharp turn to the right, followed the high hedge to an arch carved into the vegetation. On the other side was the tennis court. *Thwack!*

"Too good," announced D. A. Prescott, Jr. His sister's cross shot had steamed by his backhand to puff chalk at the court's corner. Spearbroke stood on the embankment above the court, and watched the play without speaking. A blink in Libby's concentration signaled his arrival, and her brother, as he bounced the ball readying to serve, looked at him briefly from beneath the sun-bleached eyebrows.

He bore a striking resemblance to the senator—the same elongated boniness and freckled complexion that had sustained a boyish quality in the senior Prescott's face even until his death at the age of eighty. Prescott's serve was more artful than strong and he employed a very steady baseline play; his long, muscular arm swinging with a perfect pendulum motion from the shoulder. Occasionally, if his sister were careless in return, he would shovel a squash shot just over the net, but Libby was more than a match for him. In fact, Spearbroke noted with a curious pride, she was a beautiful tennis player, and he almost applauded as she came to the net to put away Prescott's forehand with a backhand volley that was of championship caliber.

"Hi," she called, waving to him. "I'm two up on a match breaker. It won't be long."

The agent answered with a wave of hand, conscious of her brother's glare and also feeling somehow uncomfortable in his city clothes, as if he were out of uniform. The long slender legs and supple arms of both brother and sister were bronzed, their loose tennis briefs suggesting the trim athletic bodies underneath. It was Libby's serve and she had marched purposefully to the baseline, turned about, and stopped. Abruptly she clasped the racket between her slim thighs, handle to the front, and reached up to refasten the rubberband that held back the light hair in a pony tail.

Thwack! Her serve was low and inside, forcing his backhand, which she immediately volleyed at the net. She seemed to be everywhere, her feet moving moth-like, the line of muscle rippling from forearm up through shoulder and down her side and hip, aggressive and precise. Her brother lobbed defensively and she waited for it to drop, patiently, racket back, thighs tensed; then, softly tapped the point away as if shooting a butterfly.

Thwack! Her second serve was returned evenly, and they settled into a continuous baseline play that looked as if it would go on forever. It had a mesmerizing effect on Spearbroke and apparently also on Libby, for, suddenly, her brother chopped a dropshot into the forecourt, which she looked at flat-footed.

"Bastard," she muttered, though good-naturedly, and hit the spare ball at him. Prescott won his two serves and broke hers to win the tie-breaker and match. It was a remarkable turnaround. Her brother's steady strokes to the baseline seemed to entrance her so that she forgot her own net play and the one time she did come forward, and then, not aggressively but in a sort of lyrical sweep, he drove past her easily. Mercifully, he finished her off with the forehand return of a rather poor match-point serve.

"Good game," he told her as they walked toward the steps just below Spearbroke. Prescott hugged her, but she looked exhausted.

"You always do that to me," she complained.

"Not always," he countered, and his smile recalled the old senator's campaign posters. Stepping in unison, they mounted the flagstones. "Hi, I'm Doug Prescott." The hand he extended to Spearbroke was large and powerful. He was so blond that the hair on his head and his eyebrows looked white and, close up, the agent noted that his face did not tan as the rest of him. The skin between the freckles was reddish and looked tender. Spearbroke guessed he was a few years younger than his sister.

"You're coming over for a drink," she reminded him.

"Yes," he replied, and spoke to the agent. "Sorry

that I can't have dinner with you and Lib. I've got to get down to the city. But I'll see you in a bit." He turned and walked away on the path, toward the main house and his part of the compound.

Spearbroke felt awkward; he did not know how to greet Libby West now that they were alone, but she took his hand and headed them for the gate cottage. No, she had not heard anything from Hardy. She was grateful for his discreet employment of the police department. No, she didn't have the foggiest idea what information Barbara Greenburg would have discovered.

"Where is it she's vacationing?" she asked as they came to the cottage.

"A Yoga camp on Long Island," Spearbroke replied, smiling.

"How amusing. You don't suppose Hardy is doing all those funny sit-ups and things?"

"No, but perhaps he knows someone who is."

"I hadn't thought of that." Libby stopped before a wall of privet. She picked a few leaves from a branch. "I guess it has become popular." She took his arm and continued the walk. "Well, here we are."

The gate cottage was neither a cottage nor at the entrance to the estate, but was part of that straight-faced attempt by the very rich to minimize their wealth by misnomer, to refer to their summer mansions as "camps," and which probably began, Spearbroke thought, with the *petites fermes* where Bourbon shepherdesses played. The agent entered a building as large as his own brownstone in Manhattan. It was furnished with a casual harmony around notes of dark, polished wood, parchment lamp shades, and large masses of cushions and pillows covered with faded silk prints. "Give me a moment for a shower, hey?" his hostess said.

He found his room, opened his bag, and changed shirts. It was a chamber full of books, and there were large casement windows with leaded panes that looked over the tennis court and the crisscross patterns of hedgerows. A small bath adjoined. The bed looked very old and had a canopy of faded burgundy velvet. He could hear talk and laughter as he came down the stairs and followed the sound through the ground floor to the kitchen.

"Here he is," Prescott said. "Martini?"

"Yes, thank you." The man had changed to a dark green Palm Beach suit that made his burned face look even redder. Libby wore a wildly colored hostess pajama that was backless and haltered at the top, her arms bare. She was barefoot.

"Well, how's the book business these days?" Prescott asked, handing the agent a frosted cocktail.

"It's not so . . ."

"Help yourself," Prescott directed Spearbroke to the open jar of peanuts both had been eating from. "You know, Lib"—her brother turned to her. She was washing and drying salad greens at the sink. "If I can get this contract over, it should carry us through the next fiscal year. I'm sorry." He swung back to Spearbroke, sipped his cocktail. "We're hung up with business these days. It's funny, after all the good things the old man did for the unions and now they're trying to stick it to me . . . to us." His martini hand included his sister. "And the damnedest thing about it all, of course, is that I have to pow-wow with some of their chiefs tonight when I had looked forward so to chatting with you." The smooth, rapid-fire pattern of his speech wound down with the pronoun stretched to the limit of its vowels, a gesture obviously meant to suggest sincerity.

"Junior," Libby West admonished him. "Let the poor man speak. You asked him a question."

"Oh, I'm terribly sorry," her brother said, the pale eyebrows arched. He was all attention.

"That's all right," Spearbroke said. "There's nothing to say about publishing that you probably haven't read or know about already."

"Quite," Prescott agreed, a vague look in his deep-set eyes. "And what of old Hard?" he asked. Libby started, looked up quickly from making the salad. "Where is my brother-in-law, do you suppose?"

"The best of New York police are looking for him."

"Yes, so Lib told me." He looked at Spearbroke with a hesitant expression, an anticipatory curl of lip as if he were not sure about asking the next question. "And this associate of yours . . . Miss Greenburg, by name."

"What about her?"

"I hear she's rather . . . well, liberated. It is just a coincidence, I suppose, that old Hard turns up missing the same week she goes to this Yoga camp." His eyebrows had arched, the eyes flashed wickedly.

"Junior!" Libby West admonished him.

"Sorry, Sis, but we must face all possibilities."

"That doesn't even remotely approach a possibility," Spearbroke told him firmly. He felt his face flush and turned away, refused to meet the other's grinning gaze.

"No, probably not," Prescott said smoothly. "It's no secret, of course, that I never cared much for old Hard . . ."

"Oh, Doug," Libby said in dismay.

". . . however," he continued with a suave rotation

of his blond head, "the Prescott Foundation supports a number of projects and individuals and there's no real harm done, I suppose, in keeping some of it in the family."

Spearbroke was both angry and embarrassed and looked away from them, out the back door of the kitchen. It was a Dutch door, the top half open on a kitchen herb garden that looked like an illustration in a magazine.

"Just stop that. Stop that!" Libby West said to her brother, though her tone was no more angry than if she were admonishing a child for some carelessness. "This is very rude of you, Junior. And very silly."

"You're right, of course," he said quickly. "A thousand apologies." He offered peanuts to Spearbroke.

"By the way, Lib." Spearbroke turned around and was careful to speak directly to her. "While I'm here, I'd like to take a look at Hardy's new manuscript. He wouldn't mind, I'm sure. There's a publisher who is very interested in having a look at it."

"Which one is that?" Prescott asked, finishing his drink and chewing the olive. His sister had flushed and looked quickly at him over Spearbroke's shoulder.

"That's something else," she finally said. "I thought you might want to see it, but I can't find it. Hardy must have taken it with him."

"Must dash," Prescott said. "I'll try to get back while you're all still up. Oh, old Fran might look in on you later . . . if she gets the kids to bed early. Sorry to have to leave," he told Spearbroke as he took his hand. Brother and sister kissed, affectionately, as she walked with him to the front door.

Spearbroke, alone in the kitchen, sipped his martini. He heard a car door close, an engine start, and a crunch of gravel as the car pulled out of the driveway. He heard the soft padding return of Libby's bare feet upon the polished floor, and her steps seeming to quicken in tempo with his pulse as they neared the kitchen. He had just time enough to set down his glass when she was in his arms, her slender body pressed against him.

"I'm so glad you're here," she murmured. The arms that encircled his neck were surprisingly strong. Spearbroke stroked the smooth skin between her shoulders, suddenly feeling awkward because of a detachment, a distance from her that he could only close with this paternal caress. "Just as well," she said, as if to speak to his indifference. "Cynthia's still home." Then, she turned away from him abruptly and went to the oven to squeeze lemon juice over some chicken breasts. Under her breath, she reviewed her preparations, "Chicken, okay; rice, ready; salad to toss; bread in."

"This reminds me," Spearbroke said, picking up his martini again. "Detective Ryan says there was no manuscript to be found in McKendrick's apartment. The exposé of the Lindsay administration has disappeared."

"What reminded you?" Libby West asked, opening a cabinet door above the sink. "By the way, Hardy just rebuilt these cabinets last year. Aren't they nice?" and she fanned the door panel back and forth several times on its hinges as if to demonstrate its efficiency.

"Very nice," Spearbroke replied. "What you said earlier about not finding the manuscript to his new novel. That makes two manuscripts missing."

"Yes?" She looked up, puzzled.

"Well, only a coincidence, I guess. Two manuscripts gone and both authors missing or gone."

"There's something else that bothers me," she said as she took a bottle of white wine from the refrigerator. "Why did Hardy tell us he was working with McKendrick? You say this editor at Stratton knew nothing about it."

"That's not unusual," Spearbroke replied. "It's quite possible that Hardy was helping McKendrick with the book without the editor knowing about it."

"But where are all the tapes? The police apparently found none in McKendrick's apartment." She pulled out the tray of baked chicken and put it on top of the stove.

"No, they didn't. If there is something . . . something sneaky going on, perhaps someone took the tapes." His scalp prickled. "Say McKendrick's murder was planned. Whoever did that also stole the tapes and manuscript."

"But you said the editor at Stratton held a dim view of the manuscript. It doesn't sound like the sort of a document that someone would kill over. It wasn't much of an exposé apparently."

"That's only the opinion of one person," Spearbroke continued. "Perhaps there was something in it that Wallace-Corey overlooked but that others would find very damaging. Or maybe he saw a different manuscript."

"You're making it all sound very ominous, more than I had thought . . . Oh, this is Cindy." She introduced the young woman who had come silently into the kitchen. "This is Ned Spearbroke, an old friend of your father's . . . and mine."

Hardy West's daughter looked very much like him, which was not to her benefit, for those features which gave him a rugged handsomeness made her heavy boned and a little coarse. Her manner suited her appearance; sullen and uncommunicative and apparently she had pulled herself down from upstairs only for the purpose of feeding.

They ate in the kitchen at a large round table that

Libby announced Hardy had made from an old butcher's block, and there was little conversation until Libby West mentioned some of the details of Spearbroke's friendship, and the old days with Hardy West. Then the girl became very animated.

"Cynthia is wild about Dylan Thomas," her mother said.

"You knew him . . . you really knew him?" The girl turned to the agent, her eyes unhooded and bright.

"Yes, slightly," Spearbroke replied, relishing the Muscadet. "Actually, your father knew him very well." He gave the palm to West though it had not been true.

"Daddy never told me that," she moaned.

"Oh, yes. We all used to hang out at a place in the Village . . ."

"The White Horse Tavern." Libby West supplied the name.

"That's right," Spearbroke continued. "Thomas was there a lot. It was a very warm, friendly spot. Your father and Thomas and I used to match pennies for beer."

"Did he recite a lot?" the girl wanted to know. Even her slouch had disappeared.

"Who, Thomas?" Spearbroke was trying to remember the voice, the rich pronouncements. "Yes, I do remember Thomas and the owner of the place singing duets, ballads."

"Yes, Andy . . . wasn't that his name, the owner?" Libby West interjected. "Hardy had talked about him," she added, nodding to Spearbroke.

"Yes, that's right," the agent replied. "He was a big, dour-faced man and it was almost comical to see him and Thomas standing, arms around each other, harmonizing." Then, try as he could, he found nothing more to say; the contents of his nostalgia had been used up. The light that had been in Cynthia West's eyes turned down, went out, and she rose with a half-uttered apology that could as well have been an oath, and left the room. Her mother shrugged and smiled ruefully.

"It's just an age," she explained. "Let's have coffee in the library."

They had coffee and several brandies, talking about a variety of topics and all of no interest to either of them. He imagined they were waiting for Cynthia to lapse into sulky unconsciousness. The phone rang, and Libby returned after talking in a small anteroom. It had been her sister-in-law. One of the children had a bad cough and she would not be dropping over.

It was getting late. The silk pajamas brushed the air as she poured more brandy for him, and seemed to charge it with a static electricity. She turned on the stereo, located a program of chamber music, and left the room. Spearbroke thumbed through a new translation of Lucian's *Satires;* the volume had capped a column of books stacked on the floor. There were similar piles of books stacked about the library floor, all new and most of them looking unopened. He had read the same paragraph in "Fishing for Phonies" for the third time, so he put the book aside and finished his brandy. Before dinner, he had looked down the hall from his room and located the master bedroom. All was quiet on the floor above; apparently Cynthia was asleep. The door of the master bedroom was closed and as he stood before it, the sliver of light at his feet went out. Without trying the knob, Spearbroke knew the door would be locked, and he laughed silently to himself and passed down the hall to his own room. He felt strangely relieved, as if the locked door had kept him from another act of disloyalty, one more he could easily do without.

He did not know what time it was when he awoke or what it was that brought him suddenly from a dream. There had been a man's voice, loud talk, and shushing noises but whether these sounds had been in his dream or had come through the open window of his bedroom to awaken him, he could not tell. He went to the multipaned casement and looked out. The vapors of a heavy ground fog diffused the light of a full moon. The amorphous shapes of the hedges and shrubbery, the mournful exclamations of the poplars, loomed in the luminous obscurity, and just below his window and to the right lay the tennis court, a precise diagram that seemed to glow with its own energy. There was no sound save the plaintive trill of toads.

Nor was he to see Libby West the next morning. Her note on the kitchen table, with underlined apology, explained she had to drive Cynthia back to Northampton for final exams. He breakfasted on the juice, coffee, and rolls the cook set before him. The gardener drove him to the train, and on the way back to Manhattan he once more felt relieved that their trip into adultery had been completed.

He rose directly to his office in the elevator, thinking that Libby West had used the same determination he had seen her employ on the tennis court to bring their own "game" back to what it should be and he felt much better for it. When he opened the elevator door, a uniformed policeman asked him the nature of his business.

"That's Mr. Spearbroke," Mrs. Graham vouched for him. The office was a shambles, files dumped, desks pulled apart. "Oh, Mr. Spearbroke," Mrs. Graham exclaimed, "we have been pillaged!"

eight

Detective Ryan took up one corner of the leather sofa across from Spearbroke's desk, the small black notebook on one knee and a slender ballpoint pen in one large hand. There were still a few folders stacked on the long table behind the agent, though Mrs. Graham had restored much of the office's order.

"You never told me about the earlier incident with the elevator." Detective Ryan's clear blue eyes viewed Spearbroke quizzically.

"It didn't seem important enough to mention," the agent replied. When the detective smiled, his eyes lifted as if buoyed by some inner amusement. "You believe there's a connection between that elevator business and this . . . this . . ." He used his hand to indicate the ransacked office.

"Can't say," the high, wispy voice replied. "You say nothing was taken. This might indicate that the object of this search was not on the premises. The same MO was used in both cases, entry into the building was made through the service door in the rear. Do you know how long that lock has been broken?"

"I don't know . . . , we have a part-time janitor who . . ."

"Mr. Li of the Golden Dragon downstairs," Ryan referred to his notes, "says the lock has been broken for several months. He says that he informed you of the damage on two occasions, each time he sent in his rent check."

"He may have," Spearbroke said, a little flustered. "I don't pay that much attention to those things . . . I . . ."

"You just collect the rent, eh?" Detective Ryan dimpled and smiled.

"Will you have some more coffee, Mr. Ryan?" Mrs. Graham had returned with the office pot.

"I will, Mrs. Graham, and thank you very kindly," the policeman responded, bringing up the cup and saucer from the sofa cushion beside him. He had half risen to meet her.

"Now that's just a touch of milk, isn't it?" the woman offered, presenting the small carton.

"That's exactly right," Ryan almost purred. "Thank you." They seemed to have known each other for years.

"Mr. Spearbroke?" his secretary turned around and inquired.

"No . . . no more," the agent replied, a little annoyed. He watched Mrs. Graham take her leave as the detective blew on the freshly poured coffee and delicately sipped it. "It's ridiculous, I know, but I only think of front doors . . . I mean about the break-in," Spearbroke explained to Ryan's questioning glance. "I mean that night of the empty elevator business, I kept listening for the front door to close and apparently whoever it was had gone down through the basement and through the courtyard. Didn't they?" Detective Ryan said nothing, tasted his coffee once more.

"Of course they didn't need to do that at all," the policeman said finally. "It would have been easier for them just to drop over your roof out there, onto the terrace. Thieves are no different from anyone else in that if there is an easier way to get in, they'll go that way."

"But they didn't?"

"By the way," the man flipped several pages back in his book. "Did you tell me what time Mr. McKendrick called you last Friday afternoon?"

"Let's see." Spearbroke thought back to the day he had had lunch with Hardy West. "I got back here around three o'clock because—"

"Mrs. Graham doesn't keep any kind of a log, does she?"

"No . . . but I do remember I had several calls to the Coast that afternoon . . . I got back here around three . . . it must have been around four o'clock. Why?"

"I would like to talk with Mrs. West." Detective Ryan ignored Spearbroke.

"I would hope you wouldn't. She's under great strain at the moment. Besides, there's no real reason to talk to her, is there?"

"Mr. Spearbroke, as a result of a relationship you enjoy with Deputy Inspector Gambino, I have been assigned to a situation that has no head or tail to it. It is a case that is not a case."

"That's right? No crime has been committed that we know of. Well, this burglary—but is it connected to . . ."

". . . to what, Mr. Spearbroke?" Ryan's voice had thinned. "You see, I wonder why I'm here other than paying off some favor for Gambino. Your client has not shown up in Missing Persons. There are no indications of foul play. You have been broken and entered, but if you'll pardon me, the careless way you operate this address almost puts it into the category of an attractive nuisance—"

"Just a minute." Spearbroke held up his hand. "You can withdraw if you wish. If the police department does not wish to help us find Hardy West, I'm sure we can find some private agency to do the job."

"I'm sure you can," Detective Ryan said dryly, with a glint that irritated Spearbroke even more. "Now then," he continued in a friendly manner, their brief exchange behind them, "what about your assistant, Miss Greenburg? When does she return?"

"Tomorrow, I hope. She's supposed to be back tomorrow evening."

"I don't suppose this place she's at has a telephone?" Ryan said with a curious smile.

"Of course!" Spearbroke started and felt his face flush. "Mrs. Graham," he yelled.

"Yes, I heard." His secretary appeared in the doorway. "I already tried to call Barbara, but the phone seems to be out of order."

Detective Ryan turned and nodded as if to approve Mr. Graham's enterprise. "That's the same answer I got," he told her. "But," he shifted his bulk on the sofa to face Spearbroke, "we can wait to talk to her tomorrow. Have her call me when she gets in."

"Just a minute," said Spearbroke, who had listened to their talk with amazement. "You already know about the phone. Why did you ask me?"

"I just wanted to know if you had tried to call her," the detective replied, and turned over a page in his notebook. "I don't suppose you're going to give me the name of this woman who recently had an affair with West?"

"Not yet. Let's see. As you say, nothing has really happened yet." The agent fixed a cigarette in his holder, enjoying the look in the policeman's eyes.

"Incidentally," Ryan said, leaning back in the sofa. He was one of the few people, Spearbroke reflected, who made it seem average-size. "I had someone find a copy of *Sometimes, A Saturday*."

"Where did you find it?" Spearbroke asked, genuinely amazed. Hardy West's only published novel had been out of print for nearly ten years.

"I know someone at the Strand bookstore," the detective answered with a vague glance around the room. "Mr. West's a very romantic writer, isn't he?"

"Yes, you might say that," the agent replied. "You read the novel?"

"Yes. I enjoyed it," the man said simply. "I used to read a lot of poetry when I was younger, you know."

"No, I didn't know," Spearbroke replied.

From Clee to heaven the beacon burns,
The shires have seen it plain,
From north and south the sign returns
And beacons burn again.

The detective had recited with head back, eyes half closed. Spearbroke wasn't sure, but it seemed that even Mrs. Graham had paused in her endless typing of contracts to listen.

"Kipling?" the agent finally offered.

"Housman," the detective corrected.

"Of course."

Ryan transferred his coffee cup to the desktop, and closed his notebook.

"I'll have Barbara Greenburg call you when she gets back."

"I don't think there's any hurry." Ryan stood up and fixed his pen inside his jacket pocket. "If she really had anything important she would have called you. Also, since she left before West presumably disappeared, she—presumably—knows nothing about any of this."

"That's right," Spearbroke said, smiling. "That's right," he repeated, and was about to add that this idea had not occurred to him when the look in the detective's eye told him he knew that it had not occurred to him. "Well, it seems like a lot of clouds and no peaks."

"What's that mean?" Ryan asked thoughtfully.

"I mean," he got up and prepared to escort the policeman to the door, "I mean, Hardy West might not be missing, as I guess you believe, and that all these other things like this," he indicated the disarray of the office, "and McKendrick's murder *and* missing manuscripts—all those coincidentals." His voice had risen beyond what he had intended. "Who came in here and did this?" Spearbroke was suddenly outraged by the invasion. "Who did this? What were they looking for? What else but that exposé. They assumed that I would have a copy, perhaps *the* copy. I am, after all, Hardy's agent."

Spearbroke's outburst, as spontaneous as it was forceful, did not deter Detective Ryan. He moved with a ponderous grace toward the elevator, nodded courteously to Mrs. Graham, and let the door close on his smile.

"I'll be damned," Spearbroke muttered and turned back to his office. He gathered up several folders and restored them to their proper files. Whoever had sacked the place had looked carefully through every folder of every client Spearbroke represented.

"Mrs. Graham," he said, still at the files, "let's suppose you were the burglar." He turned to face her.

"Uh-huh," she replied, a little startled. The electric hum of her typewriter was switched off and she swiveled about to face him.

"What would you be looking for in this office?"

"Well, money," she suggested. She took a minute handkerchief of violet linen and touched her nose with a swift delicacy. Then she fumbled with a crushed package of cigarettes and withdrew one.

"No, not money, nothing like that," Spearbroke continued. "Whoever it was was looking for something else. These files were read nearly word for word, or so it looks. What would we have, or what might someone think we have that would cause them to look so extensively?"

"Well, maybe as you just said—the exposé." Mrs. Graham smiled and exhaled a heavy stream of smoke.

"But the editor who saw the McKendrick piece said it wasn't worth much, not much of an exposé."

"Maybe there was another one, a different one?" she suggested as her fingers lightly drummed the desktop. "Or maybe they were just looking for information we might have."

Spearbroke was turned around by her rather young laugh. "What's funny?"

"I was just thinking, why not ask Cecilia St. John? She's the expert on this sort of thing."

"What a great idea." Spearbroke closed a file drawer. "I wonder if she's free for dinner."

Several of Cecilia St. John's mysteries had been made into motion pictures. They were the favorites of the crime book clubs. So she was one of Spearbroke's best clients, though he no longer read her manuscripts. Between Mrs. Graham and Greenburg, the St. John prose was culled and spelling corrected, then sent to her publisher where it was routinely put into print and scooped off the book counters across the country.

Cecilia St. John asked Spearbroke to meet her at the restaurant in the ground floor of the small hotel where she lived in the Sixties, east of Park Avenue. The agent often wondered if any of the staff of this hotel realized that this plump, blue-haired lady was the author of such modern mystery classics as *Like a Cockroach* or *Lt. Hse. Kp. Murder,* the latter translated into a couple of dozen languages, or whether they knew her only as the widow of the late Admiral Burleigh Cinjen, one of a large flock of well-fed and pampered old birds that roosted in elegant perches on the Upper East Side.

"Now we must have another martini," she said after their second round. Spearbroke had not yet told her why he asked her to dinner and she assumed it was to talk about her new book. The restaurant was small, tastefully decorated, and the meal was going to cost him a lot. "Henri," she signaled the headwaiter, her multiringed right hand catching the candlelight to fragment the room with spectra.

"You'll like the new one—it's at the typist's." She leaned close to talk, her heavy bosom pressing the edge of the table. "I do believe I've carried the locked room a step farther."

"Up or down?" He had been a little dizzied by the quick pace she had set with the cocktails.

"Oh, Ned," she giggled throatily, "you're so sharp. How did you guess?"

"What?" he asked, confused.

"You'll see," she replied gleefully, a sharp finger testing his arm.

"Look here, Cecilia," he said after the next round of martinis were served. "I think we should order, don't you?"

"If you wish," she sounded disappointed. "You're not drinking your celery juice as I've told you. You really must take better care of yourself, Ned."

"I know," he said sincerely.

"Now look at me," she invited. "I had a nice dollop of celery juice an hour ago, and I'm in complete control of my senses." Once more the bejeweled hand had signaled the headwaiter, and Spearbroke found himself following her selection from the menu. It was only after the soup and halfway through the entrée that he felt sufficiently sobered up to talk about the whole series of incidents that had taken place after his lunch with Hardy West six days before. He omitted the afternoon with Libby.

"Wondrous, wondrous" was Cecilia St. John's response. "What do you suppose they were looking for in your office?"

"Then you think there is a connection?"

"No question about it, Ned. None whatsoever," she replied. He could tell by the glaze in her small brown eyes that a plot was being worked out. "I would so love to meet this Detective Ryan of yours. He's a rather special man, I wonder if you know."

"He seems fairly capable," Spearbroke said, trying the asparagus.

"Special." The old woman puffed and sighed. "Major Case is an elite group of professionals. All of them, if they had chosen to take the exams and do the routine paperwork, could be captains or better by now. He's one of that sort; he'd rather be a detective. But he's probably getting paid as much as a captain. I'd love to meet him."

"Well, maybe some time," Spearbroke promised.

"Two things I wonder about." She aligned her knife and fork on the plate and sipped some water, then some wine. "His question about the call from the man who was mugged—it's difficult to work without names and I supose you're not going to tell me any, no—very well . . . let's say Man A . . . He asked you what time of day Man A called you? Then there is Man B, your client, the unsuccessful novelist. Oh, dear, Ned, I didn't know you had any unsuccessful clients . . ." She paused as their plates were removed.

"We have Man A and Man B," Spearbroke reminded her.

"Yes." She leaned forward to accept the light he offered her cigarette. He lit one himself and inserted it into the holder. "Now we know, or you have been told, that A and B were supposedly working together on this manuscript, at least B told you this . . ."

"You don't believe that story."

"Forget all that." She waved the hand with the burning cigarette dangerously close to her hair. He was afraid it might ignite suddenly like magnesium. "You've been told by one editor that it was no good, and surely your own judgment must tell you that nothing interesting can be written about the Lindsay administration, now admit it."

"No, I guess not."

"There . . . you have two bits of evidence you must accept, the editor's judgment and your own intuition—both against a rather tenuous story told by Man B. You have to go with the facts."

"Yes."

"But," she hunched forward, and he pulled back quickly. It had looked as if she were about to put her cigarette out on his nose. ". . . but this is not to forsake a connection between A and B. You all knew each other years before. None of you kept up . . . well, you had your relationship with him, but I get the feeling it was no closer than you have with the rest of us. Really, now? Yes, you can't afford to be too chummy, can you? Right." She paused to test the apple tart, the cigarette still in her left hand. The ash had become quite long and finally fell onto the tablecloth. Cecilia St. John brushed it off nonchalantly.

"So there was a connection between A and B, though it might not be the ghost job on the Lindsay exposé . . ." Spearbroke enjoyed the sting of hot coffee in his mouth.

"Forget about that . . . that's all poppycock."

"Man B told me a lie about this, then. But why?"

"I would think you've been set up," she replied.

"But why?"

"Exactly. I'm sure Detective Ryan is wondering the same thing. You see, A and B do share something besides a relationship with you in the old days . . . and it is not this awful manuscript you keep bringing up. You really must get beyond thinking about manuscripts. The most obvious thing they might share would be a woman."

"But if you knew Man A, I mean how he looked, fat—it's hard to believe that he and Man B would be rivals . . ." and he laughed to think of McKendrick vying with Hardy West over a woman.

"But you haven't seen him in many years; perhaps he's taken off weight," she sighed.

"But he was a slob," he continued. That glazed look in her eyes had returned as she carefully prepared her tea with lemon and sugar.

"And you haven't talked to Man A in years, either, have you?" she asked.

"No. What are you getting at?"

"Well." She stirred, put down her spoon. "How can you be sure that you actually talked with the real Man A on the telephone the other afternoon—you hadn't talked to him in years, you said."

"No, that's right. And there was something strange about the conversation."

"Let's return to Man A and Man B." She sipped her tea. For a moment Spearbroke glimpsed her as an admiral's wife presiding over the silver service at a reception for Navy wives. "They did share something . . . whether a woman or not, and I'll accept your judgment that it was probably not that. That's another fact we must accept. For the moment it is not important precisely what it is they shared—let's call this factor X, the connecting link. A times B, so to speak." She had traced out the equation on the linen cloth with the tip of a dessert spoon.

"Now, we come to motive," she continued.

"Motive, motive for what . . .?"

"For Man A being murdered."

"Murdered, McKen . . . Man A was murdered?"

"Of course he was murdered." She smacked her lips. "That is why Detective Ryan asked you what time Man A called you. I'm sure he's already got a report from the ME—the medical examiner." She took another cigarette and waited patiently until he lit it for her. "I'll bet anything that report fixes the time of death much earlier. They can do that by the contents of the stomach, other analyses, and are awfully clever at it." She puffed a heavy cloud of smoke straight up.

"But Man B couldn't do that sort of thing . . . he just couldn't."

"It is a strange business," she said with a mournful smile. "None of us knows what the other is really like and the names we are given only confuse things more."

"So what you're saying, in a sense, is that I was actually talking on the phone with a dead man," he said finally.

"What a delicious concept," she replied, and he could tell she made a mental note. "Yes, that's what I would think, and I'm sure Detective Ryan feels the same way. Now we come back to X again, the connecting factor between A and B. That's why A was knocked off." She smiled as if to excuse the slang phrase, though her narrow shoulders moved authoritatively. "Let's introduce the break-in. Whoever broke in was looking for that connecting link, the factor X."

"To destroy it," he suggested.

"Yes, probably." She inhaled a large ball of smoke and milled its thread from her nostrils.

"Do you think he found it?"

"We can't say yet, can we? But you said *he,* just now."

"Well," Spearbroke said, with a sick feeling, "we're talking about Man B, aren't we?" Hardy West as a murderer—he felt both betrayed and full of pity.

"I'm afraid so." She had patted, then grasped his hand in a motherly fashion. "It's very logical."

"But why?"

"Factor X," she said with pursed lips. "That's all we have for now."

"I can't believe it." Spearbroke shook his head. To signal his readiness to end the evening and its speculations, he folded his napkin abruptly and dropped it beside his coffee.

"There is one thing we haven't considered," his client said idly as she turned and stared into the water glass, as if it were some sort of divining object. "Perhaps if A and B were not sharing a woman, perhaps . . . ," she lifted her well-cared-for pleasantness to his regard, ". . . perhaps they were sharing a pretty young boy." She laughed loudly, holding the edge of the table.

* * * * *

Ned Spearbroke felt frustrated and out of kilter when he returned to the sidewalk after trundling his blue-haired client to the elevator of her apartment. He needed to walk so he paced up Third Avenue, his lungs breathing deep to clear the fumes of both the heavy dinner and the new theory that had been served up.

He did not want to believe that Hardy West could kill anyone. But even more, he hated the idea that West may have set him up. After all the years of friendship, to be used by him that way—and all the while the guy had not sold a single piece in nearly a dozen years. A dozen years; Spearbroke calculated as he paused for the traffic at Eighty-sixth Street. A dozen years he had carried Hardy West, sent his manuscripts around, and then he sets him up. Maybe Libby might come up with an interpretation for the factor X, certainly one more sensible than the last one the mystery writer had suggested.

He had grown tired. Irene's was only a couple of blocks away and he thought to have a drink there and then take the long cab ride back home.

The large black woman greeted him effusively, leaving her station at the end of the bar to come forward, put her arms up and kiss his cheek. "You just missed Styron," she told him. "Are you eating?"

"No, just a nightcap," he gestured toward the bar.

There was the usual crowd; some he nodded to and others he ignored. In the mirror over the bar he saw a large party at one of the tables halfway back. Nancy Morrison was one of the group. She sat partially facing the front and on her left was her golf champion, his truck driver's back and sloping shoulders capped by a mass of curly red hair. As he sipped his Wild Turkey, Spearbroke assumed she had seen him come in. So, after a few seconds it did not surprise him to see the heavy blond hair being pulled to one side and the TV commentator's lovely face turn in his direction.

Spearbroke turned around to face her directly. Her look was serene and, he thought, meaningful. There was a slight shift of those purplish eyes to check on the attention of her escort, and when the golfer lowered his head to better feed on some soul food delicacy, Nancy Morrison chose that moment to look directly at Spear-broke and slowly stick out her tongue. No, he told him-self, Hardy West could not be a homosexual. No way.

nine

The office had been too quiet in the past week, as Mrs. Graham had observed, and Spearbroke had even more reason to lament Greenburg's absence when he found himself at a dreary cocktail party on Friday afternoon, hosted by a publisher to celebrate the publication of a client's book. Attendance at these functions usually fell to the junior member of the firm, so a murmur of speculation passed through the large reception room at Stratton Publishing when the debonair Ned Spearbroke stepped from the elevator. There must be a big deal, the rumor was already halfway around the room, something really big if Spearbroke himself showed up, though the agent's client, a popular historian whose sources Spearbroke thought doubtful, had been lucky to get any contract at all.

He moved through the crowd as if through a shallow puddle, adrift with gossip and conjecture, but his spirits were kept afloat by the expectation of calling Barbara Greenburg when she returned later on that evening. Perhaps whatever she had heard about Hardy West during her week's retreat would supply the missing X-factor that Cecilia St. John had mentioned. As he chatted with the historian and several of the Stratton people, he noticed a young man with popped eyes circling their group, apparently waiting for an opportunity to talk to him or, if the expression in the eyes were to be believed, assassinate him. The part in the young man's hair looked painful and Spearbroke could find no charitable excuse for his tie; but the expression in the eyes, the fixed stare of a junior editor studying the back of the man ahead of him, suggested that he was the person who had spoken to him about the McKendrick manuscript.

"I'm the current Dexter Corey," he said, almost taking Spearbroke's arm, "Roger Wallace."

"Hello, Mr. Wallace." Spearbroke shook hands. It was a quarter to five, he noted on a wall clock over the young editor's shoulder.

"What in hell is all this about that McKendrick manuscript, anyway?" Wallace plunged in. "I had some detective from the police department in to see me this morning about it."

"Really?" Spearbroke replied, genuinely surprised. "His name was Ryan?"

"Yes, that's right. A big Irish flatfoot right off the beat."

"He's a little more than that," the agent said offhandedly. "What did he want to know?"

"Well, he asked if I had actually met McKendrick. No, I said. The manuscript came over the transom. Had I met Hardy West? Again negative. What was the condition of the manuscript, how was it written, why didn't we offer a contract . . . he almost sounded like an agent, you know?" Wallace laughed, but laughed alone, and continued more soberly, though not without the same edge in his manner. "By the way, don't you represent Hardy West? Whatever happened to him? It's a long time between books, isn't it?" He plucked the onion from his cocktail and chewed it juicily. "I looked him up the other day; his novel was done years ago."

"Anything more?" Spearbroke looked over the other's head again at the clock on the wall. "Did Detective Ryan wish to know anything more?"

"Well, most of his questions were what the manuscript was about. Seems like it wasn't found, not even copies of it, at McKendrick's place. Do you think he was murdered?"

"Naturally, you summed up the material in your cogent fashion," Spearbroke continued.

The younger man smiled and shrugged his shoulders. "Well, what can you say about four hundred pages of old news clips rearranged into a narrative with all the verve and punch of Ford Madox Ford?" He smiled winningly.

"Not a fast read, you're saying," Spearbroke drawled.

"Exactly." Wallace's face was luminous. "Not a fast read at all. It was an incredibly bad mess, slapped together."

"Surely, Mr. Wallace, you make it sound an irresistible challenge to your gifts. That is your job here, isn't it?" Spearbroke paused to look about the carpeted, curtained, and completely featureless room. ". . . isn't that your job; to transform such artless prose into hot page-turners?"

"Yeah." The young man shook his head, unmarked by the agent's sarcasm. "But there has to be something to start with. I mean . . . this had nothing."

"You mean . . . not even marks for spelling, punctuation?"

"Okay." Wallace laughed. "Prettily typed and all that, but . . . I mean, I don't get paid enough to read stuff life that."

"So another rejection for you to hand out," the agent said.

" 'Fraid so," the young editor said, trying to smile humbly. Spearbroke wondered where he kept the score.

"Just a minute. You sent the manuscript back?"

"Yes, didn't I just say that?"

"Yes, but how did you send it back? Where did you send it back?"

"Oh, I see." Roger Wallace shaded his bulging eyes with one hand. "I don't know if I can remember. It came in by messenger, I remember that, because not many arrive that way. I had talked to McKendrick on the phone and he sent it up by messenger. Ah, that's it." He took the last of his cocktail. "He had no phone, apparently, so I couldn't call him about my reaction—just as well, I guess—and there was postage and an address for the return. It was a post office box. Yes, that's right, a post office box."

Spearbroke looked at the clock. It was a quarter after five. "We all owe you a great debt. Though perhaps," he added as he moved away, "you should give Ford Madox Ford another chance."

The historian delayed Spearbroke's departure with a hallway discussion on why the *Reader's Digest* had failed to buy his book. So it was not until five-thirty that Spearbroke was able to reach the building's lobby and a pay phone. Barbara Greenburg's answering service said she had not returned yet, so he left a message for her to call him at the Players' Club.

The Players' was nearly empty at this hour. Spearbroke went to the bar in the game room for a drink. The actor he generally played billiards with was on tour with a show, and he declined the invitation to join the game in progress, for he did not want to leave the play should his associate call. But she did not phone back, and at seven o'clock, several gins later, he dialed her number again. Yes, the answering service advised him, Miss Greenburg's messages had been picked up. No, she did not leave any messages for him. The agent was hungry, a little drunk, and hurt as well as angry with his associate's indifference. He dined alone at the club in the old conservatory.

On the way home, he walked twice around Gramercy Park before heading north. No doubt, Greenburg had had a better offer for dinner and perhaps other diversions, endeavors in which the supple gymnastics of her week's vacation could be put to use.

The brownstone was quiet, empty, and his apartment almost forbidding. All of the books, the pieces of sculpture, the large collection of records and tapes, all of his possessions so carefully collected did not interest him at the moment; no longer a last, favorite resort when friends and lovers closed their own doors. Spearbroke did not have to be alone at this moment; companionship of a sort was just a phone call away; but he reflected as he dropped his keys on the small table by the elevator that he entertained visitors whose length of stay was determined by what they wanted from him and how long it took to get it.

He poured some bourbon and put on a tape of Duke Ellington's last concert. He was weary of the printed word and fed up with those who tried to spell it. He had had enough of books and authors and publishers and sat in the corner of the big sofa and sipped the aromatic whiskey. The driving rhythm of the orchestra, the clash and color of the brass section carried him out of himself, and he let the Strayhorn arrangement lave his frustrations. At about eleven o'clock, his reverie was disturbed by a dissonance he identified as the telephone chimes. It was Detective Ryan.

"I have something bad for you."

"Yes?" Spearbroke felt the hair rise on his scalp; he could already hear what Ryan was to say.

"It's your associate, Miss Greenburg. I'm calling from her apartment. I'm afraid she's been killed. I hate to ask you, but since you're her employer, you're the closest person who can make an identification."

Numb and angry, sickened, Spearbroke let the taxi bounce him around the backseat like a stuffed doll. He felt defiled as he lay against the seat of the car as it drove him to meet Ryan. The lights of the city had dimmed and flickered. A heavy odd angled pain turned over within him as he paid the cabbie; this would be his first visit to Barbara Greenburg's apartment. It was a neat building on Eighty-second Street off Central Park West. He identified himself to the policeman at the doorway, found her apartment number on a mail box—"B. A. Greenburg"—and walked the three flights up.

Detective Ryan and another policeman in plain clothes stood on the landing outside the apartment's open door. A uniformed cop came out of the apartment and squeezed down the stairs past Spearbroke, and sporadic flashes of a strobe unit arced in the doorway as photographs were taken inside. Before he could say anything, Ryan had put an arm around his shoulders and walked him down the small hallway away from the apartment.

"I am sorry," he said. "But I figure it's better you than for her parents to see her this way."

"I understand." The agent took a deep breath and moved as if to enter the apartment, to get it over with.

"Wait a minute," the detective stopped him. The blue eyes seemed to melt, the fleshy sacks beneath them drooped mournfully. "It's going to shock you more than you think." When Spearbroke said nothing, only looked toward the open door, the policeman added, "Perversion."

"What do you mean?" Spearbroke stood apart.

"Now, now," Ryan soothed him. "I'm trying to make it easy for you. It looks like whoever she was with got carried away. It sometimes happens with this sort of thing. Are you ready?" The agent, not completely mollified, took a breath and followed the policeman.

He fell back as they passed through the small living room to register all of the details of this part of Barbara Greenburg's life, a part that he never knew. He observed the books and records, the plants in the windows, the cozy sofa, and the prints on the wall. He should have studied the furnishings and accouterments of this room at leisure some other time. He would like to have known where she collected the delicate sea shells arranged in a glassed frame of sand that made for a tabletop. Just for a second, the image of Barbara Greenburg gathering shells and small bits of driftwood on a beach stabbed him. Ryan stopped and turned around.

"All right?" he asked, and Spearbroke nodded and walked determinedly into the bedroom.

She had been bound to an armchair, exposed nakedly in a position that only death could have made more obscene and did. Her head had been encased in a black leather helmet with openings for eyes and mouth, and what looked to be a white rubber ball had been fixed between the pursed lips. The eyes bulged through the mask's openings with the same convexity as the gag in her mouth and the dog collar choker that had strangled her was fastened to the back of the chair so that the posture was erect and the small body pitifully vulnerable.

"Like I said," Ryan nodded to a police photographer who moved around this subject, "the people into this sort of thing sometimes get carried away. You all right?"

Spearbroke sat down carefully on the edge of the double bed. Some stuffed animals grazed on the cambric pasture of the bed's bolster, a bizarre contrast to the grotesque horror in the chair. He tried to look away, as if not to spy on this secret of Barbara Greenburg now revealed, openly revealed by her murderer. Feet and arms had been tied to the chair and the fine breasts whose soft shadows he had observed a few days before had been forced through a peculiar harness that pushed them out angrily, as if they were about to burst open like rotten fruit. He wondered when the gag was removed from the mouth would the scream that it stopped escape and make them deaf with its fierce agony. He finally looked away. A book of poems lay by the bed on the floor. A box of Kleenex. Parts of a manuscript—it looked like the new Noring novel—lay on the shelf of the bedside table.

"How strong is your belief in coincidence?" Detective Ryan was asking. Spearbroke, still unable to speak, shook his head. "No, I don't have much use for it, either. So, I'm putting out a warrant for your friend West, suspicion of murder. Whether the papers pick it up or not, because this has become something more than just a favor for Inspector Gambino." The light voice carried anger, and Spearbroke nodded.

"You see," Ryan continued, and Spearbroke was vaguely aware that he had moved to the body. "There's this bruise at the base of the neck, and if it turns out to be what I think, it suggests that he tapped her one first and that's wrong, because the people who do this sort of thing do it willingly."

"Yes, yes," Spearbroke sighed and picked up the

volume of poems. He did not know the author, a former professional football player who now taught English in Ohio, according to the book flap.

"How many people knew about Miss Greenburg's sexual perversions?"

"Please." Spearbroke stood up, the book of poems raised above his head. "Please!" But the insult he felt for Barbara Greenburg was quickly doused by the cool light in Detective Ryan's eyes. He seemed wound tight around an anger that surpassed Spearbroke's. "Well, it would be a long list," he finally admitted, and sat down again. "I really don't know. She was never specific about whom she was seeing. I don't think West knew her at all well, only to talk to on the phone."

"But he would know about her . . . about this sort of thing."

"Yes, I suppose so. Maybe. I don't know."

"Do you have enough?" he heard the detective ask the photographer. "All right now, Mr. Spearbroke—this gets worse." Ryan was unbuckling the hood. It was a complicated, seemingly more complicated than necessary, arrangement of zippers and straps. Then he removed the gag and lifted off the leather helmet.

Spearbroke felt his stomach become stone. He stared into a Medusa, the hair pulled up and away by the hood's removal, the face contorted in the final agony. The popped eyes held his gaze with blind ferocity and the open mouth screamed at a pitch that only his soul could hear.

"My God!" He felt his stomach heave and turned away, gasping for breath. The detective helped him to a chair.

"That is not Barbara Greenburg," he finally managed to say. "Whoever she is, poor woman, she is not Barbara Greenburg."

ten

"This is Detective Kraft." Ryan introduced the sallow-faced man beside him, perhaps a few years younger, and with a large curved nose that threatened to hook his upper lip. Spearbroke and the two detectives sat at a table in a room at the Twentieth Precinct Headquarters. The air-conditioning was running, and Ryan hunched over the table resembling, Spearbroke thought, an Irish conspirator about to convey the secrets of British troop movements.

"He's your alibi." Ryan shrugged and threw his head toward his partner.

"My alibi!" Spearbroke was hurt, astounded that anyone would think him guilty of anything.

"After your assault, Detective Kraft made sure you got home okay at nights."

"I see," the agent said, and wondered if he should thank the man for his protection, but the detective presented a disposition of such sourness that he decided it was wiser to say nothing.

"You were never ... never intimate with Miss Greenburg?" Ryan asked mildly.

"Never," Spearbroke replied. Even at this late hour, the police station clattered and rang with activity. The door to their small conference room was partway open. "Where is she? Shouldn't we ... *you* send out some sort of an alarm?" and the look in the detective's eyes silenced his advice. But Ryan smiled.

"We've contacted her parents in Sheepshead. She went to see them last evening on her way back from Yoga camp. Took them out to dinner at a restaurant nearby, visited for several hours, and then took the late train into the city. She would have arrived about an hour ago." He held a hand up. "Yes, we had someone at the station. He either missed her or she didn't arrive."

"So she's alive." Spearbroke took a deep breath and fished for cigarettes in his jacket pocket. He had forgotten his holder and the heavy smoke of the plain cigarette stung his palate.

"What's that you're smoking?" Detective Kraft asked suspiciously.

"Here," Spearbroke showed him the package. "They're French. And where is Hardy West?"

"Not anywhere we know of," Ryan replied.

"It seems we hardly know one another." Spearbroke felt drained.

"*All things counter,*" Detective Ryan said wistfully. He had paused but when the literary agent gave no sign of recognition, the policeman rounded out the line, lifting his pink and silver countenance to almost croon, "*All things counter spare, strange / Whatever is fickle, freckled (who knows how?)* . . ."

"Oh, yes," Spearbroke fell in, ". . . *dazzle, dim* and so on. Hopkins," he guessed.

"Right, and none of them knew *him* a poet," Ryan waxed, leaning even closer. His partner looked away, as if for a corner in which to fit his nose. "They all thought he was only a priest, and a Jesuit at that." A police sergeant came through the door with some papers.

"Here you go, Francis." He gave them to Detective Ryan. "You fellas want some coffee or something? Lissen, we're honored to have Major Case paying us a call up here."

"Yeah, yeah," Ryan said softly. No one wanted coffee. "Tell him what you have," he said to his partner after the sergeant left.

Kraft took out a notebook identical to the one that Spearbroke had seen in Ryan's hand. While the policeman found a certain page in his notes, Spearbroke spoke to Ryan. "So your name's Francis?" The white-haired detective nodded and continued to review the report that had just been given him.

"Your friend West made some interesting financial transactions lately," Detective Kraft said. He spoke from the corner of the mouth, the words connected by a slangy elastic of urban syntax. "A month ago, March twenty-first to be accurate, Sloane and Pierce—a bond and securities firm long associated with the Prescott family—sold two hundred fifty thousand worth of New York City issue for middle-income housing, these were negotiable bonds; you know, anyone who has them can cash them. Mr. West made the arrangements to sell by phone. The receipts were sent and returned by mail and the check for like amount mailed to a box number in the Chelsea Post Office. Those were the instructions West gave."

"Chelsea." Spearbroke tapped his cigarette ash. "That was McKendrick's postal zone?" Both detectives nodded, Ryan still reading the typed sheet before him.

"Suspect also . . ." Kraft had continued, but had stopped at Spearbroke's short exclamation.

"It's only an expression," Ryan soothed him. "It gives anonymity before the guilty are finally judged."

"The suspect," Kraft went on dryly and with a side glance at his partner, "also took out several thousand dollars—fifty-five hundred to be exact—from a joint checking account he shared with his wife. Then, and this is interesting," the detective's nose seemed to dip even more toward his lip, "Mr. West had made reservations, again on the telephone, for a flight to Rio de Janeiro. Pan American."

"Ah." Spearbroke puffed, getting caught up in the narrative. "The classic escape route."

"You might almost say trite." Detective Ryan's look conveyed chastisement. He had finished with the report and sat with large hands interlaced.

"Yes, trite," Spearbroke had to agree. "You said reservations. Plural."

"Right." Kraft pulled at his nose. "In his name and the other for his wife. Immigration reports a new passport issued to Mrs. West, or in her name, but it was not Mrs. West's picture." At this point, the detective pulled away a small Xerox copy of a photograph that had been clipped to his notebook and handed it, without looking, to his partner as he continued to read from his notes. Ryan looked at it casually, then handed it on to Spearbroke, who looked at the woman's face while Kraft continued his special litany.

"Subject is female, in her late twenties, dark hair, brown eyes, of central or northeastern Mediterranean extraction, possibly Italian or Greek. Ears pierced, and wears contact lenses, due to myopic condition. Tendency to be overweight, but indications of diet control."

"Know her?" Ryan asked.

Spearbroke shook his head and returned the picture. "When was this flight supposed to leave?"

"Last Saturday. Four o'clock in the afternoon."

"Last Saturday!" Spearbroke exclaimed. "Last Saturday? Then West had planned all this before he had lunch with me? Is that what you're saying?" The two men regarded the agent silently; only a slight crinkle around Ryan's eyes suggested a joke had been played. "That bastard," Spearbroke muttered. "That bastard. Why? But wait . . . he didn't go?"

"No, the tickets were never used," Ryan told him. "They also had been sent to the box number in Chelsea. They had been charged to a credit card."

"I can't get over it," Spearbroke said helplessly. "And I don't understand any of it."

"The victim tonight has been identified," Ryan said, picking up the report. He looked over the page at Spearbroke. "A neighbor in the building saw the door open, found the body, called the cops. We were called when the apartment was found to be in Miss Greenburg's name. We have all of your names on a bulletin," he seemed to apologize. "We just assumed it was her and hadn't made any more of an ID. But," he returned to the sheet, "her name was Gloria Benson, about twenty-seven years of age, and a resident of Des Moines, Iowa. She had a reservation for there on a flight that is to leave," he looked at his watch, "later this morning—eight o'clock."

"What was she doing there? Where did she come from?" Spearbroke asked. Ryan shrugged his shoulders.

"She had a small suitcase—our preliminary investigation assumed it belonged in the apartment," blue eyes glanced up toward the ceiling, "and with only the number of articles that would suggest a short trip."

"Also, one might hope she had normal sexual tastes," Spearbroke said, sorry immediately for his words because of the toughness that suddenly seized Ryan's features. It seemed to be the detective's turn to be angry. No one said anything for several moments. A phone rang continuously in the squad room outside and Spearbroke wondered why it wasn't answered. "Well, what next?" he finally said.

"We'll take you home," Ryan said, gathering his papers together and stuffing them in his coat pocket. His partner had already got up. "You're not to say anything about this to anyone, particularly about this case of mistaken identity. The perpetrator thought this was Miss Greenburg tonight. What I'm saying is that you might be in danger, too, if the murderer learned of his mistake, and that perhaps you now know whatever it was your associate is supposed to know about Hardy West."

"What could it be?" Spearbroke asked as they walked out of the police station. "What could it be that's so awful that it brings a person to murder?"

"It would probably mean nothing to us, seem very unimportant." Ryan opened the rear door of the black Dodge double parked on Eighty-second Street in front of the station. "But to the murderer, taken in the context of another life, it becomes very threatening."

"I have a client, Cecilia St. John—perhaps you've read her mysteries, or maybe detective stories bore you." The agent paused, but Ryan said nothing, attended him politely. Kraft turned the engine over. "Well, she believes," Spearbroke continued, "that there was some link between Hardy West and McKendrick. That they shared something besides the so-called exposé they were working on, and that if this factor were . . ."

"Why don't you cut through the park at Seventy-ninth?" Ryan asked his associate. He apparently had lost interest in the St. John theory.

"There's a place down here I just want to check out," Kraft said as he drove them down the middle of Columbus Avenue.

"I'm sorry." Ryan turned back to the backseat. "I'm not familiar with his work." Spearbroke didn't bother to correct him and they drove in silence, save for the occasional squawk of the car's radio bleeping messages and commands.

There was something insular and privileged about looking at this scene from within the police car, and Spearbroke smiled wryly. It was just like one of Cecilia St. John's novels.

"Big business tonight," Detective Kraft said as they passed the park and sidewalk behind the Museum of Natural History. The agent could see clusters of darker shadows, moving within the umbra of the trees; parts breaking off to join other groups, single units circulating to merge with others. It resembled a dramatization of malignant cells. Detective Ryan had only grunted and looked away.

"What is that?" the agent asked.

"Sort of a drug exchange." Ryan spoke over his shoulder. "Dealers come from around to establish the supply and set price."

"But why . . . you're right here. Why don't you do something?" Spearbroke asked as the car continued its easy momentum. He was even more surprised by their amusement.

"He wants to get us killed," the driver said with a light scorn.

"It's not our territory," Ryan explained and was about to say more when his partner interrupted him.

"Take a look," Kraft said. The car had slowed but still moved smoothly as they passed a row of storefronts and small businesses, all dark except for what looked to be an abandoned Greek restaurant. An old plastic canopy still staked a claim on the sidewalk before the dimly illuminated front and the name of the place, A E S O P S, could yet be read on the windows, but a new name had been painted on both the canopy and the windows: INTERRACIAL HAVEN OF TRUTH. Both detectives observed the establishment intently. A steel gate had been pulled across the alcove beneath the canopy and a blue light bulb burned in the enclosed area.

"What was that?" Spearbroke asked as the car speeded up. He looked through the rear window; not a person was to be seen.

"It's an after hours place," Ryan explained.

"Was there something wrong with it? Why did you want to check it out?" he asked the man at the wheel.

"You might say," Ryan answered for his partner, "he was looking for a light in the window."

Something on the radio prevented further explanation if, indeed, the detective had intended to say more. Spearbroke had not even heard the radio. "Four-three to Center," Ryan answered casually. He held the microphone close to his mouth.

"Right, four-three." The voice came clearly from beneath the dashboard. "Sixth Precinct has a couple of witnesses to the nine-o-two you've been following in Chelsea. Perpetrator described as juvenile, about fifteen years, slight build, Hispanic. Robbery. Over."

"Four-three—Center," Ryan spoke into the palm of his hand. Spearbroke had leaned forward on the seat between them. Kraft had turned east at Columbus Circle. "Do you have a time?"

"Hold, four-three." The radio went dead as the car neared the Plaza Hotel and the three continued to ride in silence across Fifth Avenue. Manhattan seemed like a small town at this hour of the morning. At the corner of Lexington Avenue, the police car turned south. There were three prostitutes, one of them very pretty, strolling along the far sidewalk.

"Four-three—Center."

"Four-three—check."

"We got no good time. Victim was found at five-fifteen P.M. One witness puts the assault around four, another at three-thirty. ME says it could be within a two-or-three-hour bracket. Check?"

"Check. Four-three, out." Ryan leaned forward and replaced the microphone. He said nothing, looked through the windshield at the empty avenue, and Spearbroke could not see his face, but his pose suggested contemplation. "Well, it looks like McKendrick was actually mugged by someone in his own neighborhood. A kid."

"A coincidence," Spearbroke supplied.

"Yes." Ryan spoke slowly. "His death was a coincidence, that seems to be true, but not the ransacking of his rooms. Not likely a kid would risk being trapped like that—not in the afternoon. That makes your phone call from him, whoever pretended to be him, the coincidence because McKendrick must have already been dead by then."

"We know that," Spearbroke said, leaning across the seat back. "We know that, but does anyone else?" He saw the silhouette of the policeman's head nodding. "Hardy West wouldn't know it was an accident, would he? What if he didn't believe in coincidences, either? What if he thought McKendrick was killed by whomever he feared? That's why he didn't take that plane. Maybe what he was telling me at lunch was true after all?" The agent spoke rapidly as all parts of his theory materialized. "There *was* something in that manuscript."

"I'll be interested to ask him when we find him—if we ever do," Ryan said softly. They had pulled up before Spearbroke's brownstone. "Now, if you'll permit me," the large detective said as he got from the car, "I'll just look over your premises before we say good night."

* * * * *

Ned Spearbroke lay in the down-filled comfort of the antique bed, physically exhausted but his mind still jogging a quick pace. Detective Francis Ryan had left after thoroughly searching the office and the apartment, with instructions about the door locks that were almost paternal but so kindly given that Spearbroke was more comforted than offended. He could not fall asleep. The awful image of that young woman murdered in Barbara Greenburg's apartment was burned into his mind. He turned over and switched on the radio; it was permanently tuned to a station that played classical music around the clock, and the room's blackness was portioned by the sweet harmony of a chamber ensemble. It was either Haydn or Mozart, he could not tell which, but the baroque variations were removed by much more than mere time from the horrors of the past week. There was a difference of civilizations. That wasn't true, Spearbroke scolded himself for his sentimental lapse and shifted once again. The Vienna of Mozart's day was a dangerous place, as many if not more muggings and murders, foot-pads they were called then. And women were savaged and friends were betrayed. Yes, certainly friends were betrayed. But in spite of all that, some men were compelled to construct such beauty as the music on the radio. Even now, he thought, there was a poem or piece of music being composed that would transcend all of this night's brutality. It would have to be a masterpiece. He turned on his back and looked into the blackness above him. A trapezoid of light passed like a spectral kite across the room's ceiling; like the lights of a passing car. But he had pulled the drapes on the front windows. Quickly, he turned down the radio. The elevator hummed. It had already passed the apartment level and went up to the office where it stopped and the dynamo clicked off.

He listened. He turned the radio off completely and listened. There was no noise. The elevator remained at the office level. He got up and put on a robe. The silk was cool upon his skin and raised goose bumps, but the heft of the hawthorn cane felt right as he lifted it off a chair. At the back of the large dressing closet was a door that opened on to the old service stairway of the original mansion. He gradually felt his way up the stairs, his hand edging around some molding and then the division between door and jamb and closing around a doorknob that jugged into the dark. He would be at the office level, outside a door that opened into his office, if it did open; he could not remember if it was locked. It was rarely used. He put his ear against it. There was a strange drumming noise on the other side. The doorknob turned easily as he remembered the fire marshals checking this escape route when they had inspected the building some months back. As far as he could tell, his office seemed undisturbed and the French windows were closed. Mrs. Graham had probably locked up before she left for the weekend. He knew the way through the office like a blind man and he easily negotiated the desk and sofa, the clutter, step by step with the cane held before him like a divining rod. There was a light in the bathroom. Someone was using the shower.

Spearbroke stationed himself outside the door of the bathroom. He held the cane in both hands, like a batter about to take up his stance in the box. The shower was turned off. There were final drips of water and the scrape of curtain hooks along a metal rod.

Then nothing. The door opened. The light in the bathroom outlined a figure against the steam.

Simultaneously with the sound of the cane hitting the floor, he heard Greenburg's twang. "Oh, boss, it's you."

"My God! It's you . . . it's you, Greenburg, it *is* you." She had wound a towel around her hair like a turban but it was all she wore and there was something so touching, so piquant about her standing nude before him that he took her in his arms with a joyous sense of relief. "You're alive. You're alive," he laughed, feeling her cool, damp body against him.

"Well, sure," she said against his chest and then pushed away as if suddenly aware of her nudity and of his beneath the robe. But his arms banded her small waist. "Wait a minute," she said. "Boss. Hey, boss. Well, good night." She sounded embarrassed, uneasy. Her breath caught as Spearbroke kissed her neck, his mouth following the freshened path along the cool skin to the delicate shell of ear. He bent over her. Finally, her arms slipped around his neck and she hung on him, her body arched against him. His robe fell apart. "Oh, Boss," she murmured. Her face turned slowly toward his.

"Oh, Greenburg," he said as their lips met.

* * * * *

They lay on the floor where they had slipped apart in a tender parody of wrestlers catching breath. With the back of his hand he brushed the smooth turn of the thigh she rested against his hip.

"Who was Gloria Benson? he asked gently. "Why was she in your apartment?"

"Oh, Gloria," she sighed. "How awful. How ugly. She was at Yoga camp. A nice person. She had this early plane to catch back to Des Moines. I gave her my apartment keys so she wouldn't have to pay for a hotel. I went by to see my parents and got back very late. I saw the lights on in my apartment, saw cops all over the place, and called a neighbor to see what was going on. The first instinct you develop in Brooklyn when you see cops around is to assume something is bad and it has something to do with you."

"The murderer thought Gloria was you; you were supposed to have been the victim." He felt her tremble and she placed an arm over her eyes.

"But why?" she finally said huskily. "Why would anyone want to kill me?" She sounded wounded, child-like. "And why like that?"

"It was supposed to suggest an accidental death during one of your . . . one of those . . . well. Listen, Greenburg, do you really go in for that sort of thing?"

"You've got to be kidding." She turned quickly. Her loose hair fell over him. The turban had fallen away some time before and his bare shoulder was dappled by ambiguous sensations. "You think I'm some kind of a nut? Who would do such a nasty thing to a nice girl like that?"

"Someone who thought he was doing it to you because you have . . . well, you talk as if you have had many experiences along that line."

"Oh damn . . . damn . . . damn," she muttered and put her arms behind her to lean on her hands. "All that shit talk. It was only meant to be for fun. A pose. Just a . . ."

"Listen, my dear," Spearbroke adopted a fatherly tone as he tapped her on the knee, "Gloria Benson would be dead no matter how you talked or fantasized. How she was killed is secondary. Her murderer wanted to kill you because you learned something about Hardy West."

"But what did I learn about Hardy West?" Her voice raised. "Nothing. I learned nothing about Hardy West. This other broad that Gloria Benson and I shared a room with, Rose, confided that she knew this writer. This was after I had said I worked in an agency."

"You didn't say which one?"

"No." She bent her legs beneath her, pulled the hair over one shoulder, and leaned sideways on one arm in a half odalisque posture. "No, you don't get close at Yoga camp," her voice drawled. "Actually, Rose said she wasn't so much interested in Yoga at all, but it was a way of getting away from this guy—Hardy West—who wouldn't go away and had even planned this crazy trip for the two of them."

"To Rio de Janeiro."

"Yeah," Barbara Greenburg said, surprised. "He had even got passports for them and had fixed one for her as his wife—in his real wife's name, and this was when old Rosie got scared because, as she said, he was married to a very important family. Rose has all the ambivalent feelings of inferiority and/or scorn the lower class has for the upper."

"Let me describe her a little more realistically," Spearbroke said dryly, and sat up, crossing his legs under him. "Your friend Rose is about twenty-seven years old, with a tendency to be plump, dark hair . . ."

"Right" came his associate's amazed voice.

". . . myopia, probably wears contacts, has had her ears pierced, and is probably of either Italian or Greek ancestry."

"Italian. Rose Donato. What's going on? How do you know all of this?"

Spearbroke told her of the last several hours he had spent with the police and referred to all that had happened since she had left—McKendrick and the missing manuscript, the office being torn up.

"So what you did learn about Hardy West was Rose Donato," Spearbroke concluded. She traced the outline of his profile with a fingertip. "Hardy has never met you?" Spearbroke sounded very sad.

"No," she answered, her voice even sadder. "Son-uv-a-bitch," she added softly, her hand rested on his chest. "He killed poor Gloria, thought he was killing me, just because I had found out he had shacked up with Rose Donato? That's crazy."

"There's more to it," Spearbroke replied. "There must be. What about the link with McKendrick?"

"But the police say McKendrick's murder was accidental, he really was mugged by a thief." She knelt in front of him in the darkness.

"But there's the manuscript, the exposé that doesn't exist. What of that?" Spearbroke stretched out against the carpet. He was very tired. "What does Rose Donato do?"

"She teaches at C.C.N.Y."

"What? What does she teach?"

"I don't know. Something in the business college." Barbara Greenburg's hand stroked his rib cage, moved lower.

"What does she do for Hardy West?" Spearbroke murmured.

"Vell, darlink, vhat do you tink she does?" Her fingers tweaked him. He pulled away.

"Be serious."

"You want me to be serious?"

"I mean . . ."

"There's a sweet young woman who's been trussed up like a turkey and slaughtered in my apartment and it could have been me—it was meant to be me. Now I can get goddamned serious about that, if you want," and she stopped talking suddenly, as if she had run out of breath.

Spearbroke sat up and took her by the arms to pull her face to his shoulder. She held one of her hands against her chin, the thumb pressed against her lips.

"Goddamn all of you bastards," she said brokenly and drew away, pulling her hair around the other shoulder and wiping at her eyes. "Ask me more questions? I'll be all right." Spearbroke took one of her hands between both of his.

"The thing about Rose Donato and Hardy West is that . . . well, as I've discovered, he was carrying on with a variety of women and all of them very classy. He had had affairs with some of the most glamorous women around, so why Rose Donato?"

"Piggy-piggy," she scoffed, but her spirits seemed to lift. "Maybe it was more than screwing for him—there are such things, I'm told."

"How did they meet? Did Rose tell you?"

"No." She raised her knees and hugged them. "Well, they didn't actually meet. He answered an ad."

"An ad?"

"Yeah, she runs a typing service out of her apartment."

"That's it!" Spearbroke jumped up, the adrenaline of discovery flushed his fatigue. "The X factor. That's what McKendrick and Hardy West shared—a typist." He stopped short and struck his brow. "My God."

"What?" The woman also stood up, for her employer turned on the small lamp and had begun to rummage through Mrs. Graham's desk.

"Look for a business card with the name of a typing service on it," he told her. The two naked members of Spearbroke, Inc., sorted through all the papers that

Mrs. Graham had placed neatly on her desk, in the baskets and drawers and receptacles of her province. Spearbroke told Barbara Greenburg about the mysterious empty elevator. "I thought the card had been stuck in the panel sometime before. But just maybe . . . maybe."

"Is this it?" the young woman asked. She looked at a small card in her hand.

"Let's see," Spearbroke said, coming to her. He looked over her bare shoulder. "Yes, that's the card I found stuck in the control panel of the elevator. *R & D Typing Service*—Rose Donato."

"She lives on the West Side, too, near me. So?"

"So, find Rose Donato and I bet we find Hardy West." Spearbroke suddenly frowned. It was like one of those exposure dreams in which the dreamer is suddenly aware that he is naked in a crowded theater lobby. But this was no dream. He looked at Barbara Greenburg's near-perfect breasts, the curve and dimple of hip. He sucked in his bare belly and looked down at himself as if to confirm his reaction to their situation. Then, he reached over and turned off the desk lamp.

"Why'd you do that?" she asked, amusement in her voice. The light of dawn had passed through Brooklyn and was about to cross the East River.

"Look here, Greenburg." He spoke to her silhouette. "I hope you'll understand and forgive my behavior a little while ago. That grisly scene in your apartment, and I was so worried about you. I was very worried."

"That's nice," she said, coming to him. "That's nice."

"But I want you to understand," he continued, "my emotions just got the better of me."

"That's very nice," she said once more. She had

come quite close and stood before him. Her breath caressed his chest. "But then we have this company policy, don't we?" she intoned. "No intradepartmental screwing, right?"

"Yes, that. But I don't want you to think I was taking advantage . . . but I was so relieved to see you. I mean," and he laughed abruptly, "there you were."

"Sure, Boss, I understand." She spoke quietly. She still stood before him, arms at her sides. The early light through the windows illuminated her bare shoulders, the curve and flare of her back. "I'd better go."

"Go? Where will you? Your life is in danger. You mustn't leave. You'll have to stay."

She had slowly lifted her arms around his neck as he spoke and he drew her against him, and stroked her back. It was a gesture that went beyond the paternal. "I guess I'm just trapped here, aren't I?"

"It wouldn't be safe for you to leave." He kissed her in the middle of the forehead. Then he kissed the bridge of her nose. "I can't, in good conscience, let you leave."

"But company policy, Boss," she murmured, raising her lips.

"This is an emergency," he replied. "The rules will have to be waived."

* * * * *

Too many people believe that the ubiquitous and sordid pigeon is the only bird that frequents the isle of Manhattan. This is not so. The dedicated ornithologist can enjoy a variety of avian studies, but he must rise very early or go to bed very late. There is a magic hour, just before the whine of the garbage truck compactor, when the city sings with a multitude of species that would have impressed John James Audubon. The call of the robin, the nagging chirp of wren and nuthatch, the inquisitive shrill of the finch—to name some of the most common. There are even reports that the highly overrated warble of the mockingbird has been heard in certain areas of the East Side. But one must listen carefully, and if, on this particular morning one had been listening carefully, the full feathered cries of the junior member of the firm of Spearbroke, Inc., would have been heard to join the chorus.

eleven

"I wish you had told me about this sooner," Francis Ryan said as he looked at the small card once more. He made the leather chair in Spearbroke's living room seem small. The agent noted the detective's gray wool suit had been well tailored; he was surprised by this fact and chagrined that he would be surprised.

"It didn't seem that unusual," Spearbroke replied. He sat across from the policeman to tie his shoelaces. Ryan arrived within minutes after he had left a message for him, as if he and his partner had been parked around the corner. "We must get dozens of those announcements a week. Mostly stuffed in the mailbox or stuck in the elevator just like that one. I thought it may have been left there earlier in the day."

"She probably had a cab waiting. There's a train at nine-forty for Long Island and a stop near the Yoga camp."

"Yes, Miss Greenburg said Rose Donato arrived late the first night."

"By the way, will she be much longer, do you suppose?" Ryan's eyes glanced upward, to the office floor above.

"I guess she took a shower," Spearbroke alibied for his associate. "I can't imagine she had a very comfortable night on the office sofa," he said, and looked away.

"I imagine not," Detective Ryan replied evenly. Spearbroke bent forward again to loosen and retie his shoelaces. Neither man spoke for some time.

"So." Spearbroke sat up. "Rose Donato sneaked away from Hardy, came by here on her way to the station and left this card, thinking I might call the number and discover him there. Is that your theory?"

"I don't have a theory," Ryan's voice sounded as if he, too, had been up all night. "But it does explain why there was no typewriter in McKendrick's apartment. By the way, a suspect in his killing has been detained, and a ring with his initials engraved on the band was found on the suspect. Did you know McKendrick went to Harvard? It was a class ring." The policeman seemed impressed.

Spearbroke shook his head. "That's what I think, too—that McKendrick used Donato to type his manuscript."

"And all of his letters," Ryan suggested. "His letters to the editor. His handwriting was poor and typed letters apparently are more likely to be used by newspapers." The elevator machinery commenced and they both turned toward the opaque door across the room. It slowly illuminated, the hum stopped, and the door opened.

Barbara Greenburg stepped out. She carried a small canvas bag and wore yellow slacks and a white tank shirt. An orange scarf was tied around her hair; several strands of pumpkin seeds were wound around her throat. "Well, good morning," she said, a bit too heartily, Spearbroke thought.

"Barbara, this is Detective Ryan," the agent introduced them. He noted the policeman's eyes pass over the young woman's bare arms to observe her breasts beneath the thin shirt.

"Sorry to meet you under such circumstances,"

Ryan said as he shook hands. He put on his hat and moved them back toward the elevator. "Your apartment has been cleaned up," he told her. "The Benson family will arrive later today."

"I'd like to talk to them," she said as they got in the elevator.

"I think they would appreciate that." The detective nodded and looked at her once more, this time in the face. "In the meantime, I think you should stick with us. We can put you under surveillance. It was very, very wise of you to come here last night."

"I think it was, too," Barbara Greenburg replied, her eyes wide and luminous. Spearbroke stared straight ahead. "Do you think it would be a good idea if I stayed here again tonight?" she asked the detective. Her face was a mask of concern.

"It would be easier for us to keep you both protected under the same roof. What do you think, Mr. Spearbroke?" Ryan asked as the elevator door opened.

"I think we can arrange something." He strode down the hallway. Barbara Greenburg hum-hummed under her breath.

Detective Kraft was waiting at the curb, behind the wheel of a sparkling new sedan. "Where's the old Dodge?" Spearbroke asked. He was disappointed it was a different car. "Have the fortunes of the New York City Police Department risen?" He and Barbara Greenburg sank into the luxuriant plush of the backseat.

"Not exactly," Detective Kraft replied. "We've permitted Hertz to put us into the driver's seat. You see," he continued, pulling into the traffic on Park Avenue, "a man of Detective Ryan's age begins to have kidney problems . . . and all those bumps in that old Dodge. You understand?" He had not looked at Ryan who, in turn, showed no expression. "And then," Kraft said, pulling on his nose reflectively, "I don't feel so good myself." At this his partner laughed abruptly.

"You mean to tell me, a taxpayer," Barbara Greenburg's voice was strident, "that you guys rent these cars?"

"I didn't say we rented it," Kraft said smoothly, cutting across a lumbering truck and beating out a taxi. "We've only borrowed this vehicle from an agency for whom we've done a few favors. Where on Seventy-seventh Street?" he asked his partner.

"Between Columbus and Amsterdam—one eighty-seven. There's no hurry. I put a surveillance on it when I got the address. If anything was to happen, it's already happened."

Spearbroke patted his associate's hand to comfort her, for she had turned to him quickly at the detective's words. "It's not uncommon for writers to have typists do their final manuscripts." He spoke to the detective's tight white cap of hair. Almost lazily, Ryan turned around and leaned over the seat. "And if McKendrick couldn't type—well. But why would she want me to find West in her apartment?"

"I told you why already," Barbara Greenburg replied. The fragrance of her perfume radiated within the car. "Rose told me she was trying to get rid of West, but he wouldn't go away."

"I see what you mean," Ryan said, his eyes sparkling. "It's an old trick, like calling the cops to close down one of your own parties that has got out of hand."

"But I still don't see the attraction she has for him, when he can have—well, I don't see it," Spearbroke said.

"Well, maybe as a writer," Ryan suggested, "he wants to have his own private typist."

"Ha." The young woman held up an index finger.

"He's right. I know he's right. Listen," she jabbed Spearbroke in the ribs, a bit too familiarly he felt, "Ryan knows more about writers than you do."

It was a smooth, quick ride and Kraft double-parked opposite the entrance to a converted brownstone. The police officer on duty reported there was no activity; it was Saturday morning and most of the tenants were sleeping late. On the bell panel in the foyer, apartment 3-B was listed for "R. Donato." With Spearbroke and his associate close behind, the two detectives turned to the modern all-glass front door. "Shouldn't we ring the bell?" Greenburg asked.

The policeman seemed not to hear her question. The door was operated by a key from the outside and a panic bar fitted to the inside, the whole unit set in a jamb of extruded aluminum. Almost without pausing, Kraft pressed both hands against the door around the lock face. There was a faint rasp and a click and the door swung wide open. "Cheap crap," the detective said scornfully. "No wonder we got such a high burglary rate in this town."

Both policemen went up the steps, almost in tandem, leaving the two literary agents behind. Greenburg's seed necklaces rattled as she jogged up the steps two at a time with Spearbroke moving quickly behind her. The detectives had already rung the bell for the rear apartment when they made the third-floor landing. Ryan pushed the button once more. They could hear the buzzing from inside. He tried it a third time as his partner's eyes seemed to ask something. The large detective then sighed and ran a hand through the wave of silvery hair. He glanced at the couple beside him, almost guiltily, then nodded. "Okay."

Detective Kraft pulled a small plastic card from his coat pocket and worked it between the edge of the door and the molding at the lock. "Hey, just a minute."

Greenburg's outrage had no effect. "That's illegal," she said, suddenly sounding more sorrowful than angry. Kraft had smiled at her outburst; Ryan remained impassive and seemingly impatient. With one hand on the doorknob and the other manipulating the card, the hook-nosed detective coordinated his efforts and the door swung open with a light creak.

Now the policemen proceeded slowly, one step at a time, into the apartment. Over their shoulders, Spearbroke and Greenburg could see a high-ceilinged room with a marble manteled fireplace and two large windows overlooking the back garden. It was sparsely furnished but there were three electric typewriters set up on a long table made of an unfinished door and saw horses. The machines were switched on and hummed like a trio warming up for a concert. There was paper rolled into each and a manuscript beside each, so that Spearbroke was almost certain they had intruded, that Rose Donato had only just stepped from the room, and might reappear at any moment. And indeed, a gray cat did come in quickly from the kitchen and began to rub against their legs, crying fiercely.

"Nothing's to be touched," Ryan said softly, but there was no real attempt to conceal his voice. Against the far wall, under and around the windows, an elaborate bookcase with window seats and small cabinets was half constructed. Raw lumber leaned against the adjoining wall, as if waiting its turn to come under the sharp teeth of the new-looking circular saw on the floor. There was a red metal tool box, obviously not new, opened to offer a selection of chisels, screwdrivers, and hammers. Boxes of small hardware were stacked by the radiator. The cat continued to cry.

One typewriter held a half page of what looked like a psychology thesis, and a second contained a piece of fiction. Apparently, Spearbroke thought, the professional typist rotated her chores in order to avoid boredom. But it was in the third machine that they found the message; the buzzing of the typewriter seemed to etch the words into their comprehension:

FOR GIVE US

Kraft had gone directly into the bedroom and returned as they stood over the typing bench. Carefully, he picked up the telephone in his handkerchief and dialed a number while he looked at his partner. His head slowly twisted toward the bedroom.

The woman on the bed would have seemed to be asleep were it not for the small black hole near her left ear. She looked older to Spearbroke than her picture, but her eyes had been attractive in a face that was strongly molded. The hair was dark and thick and her figure might have been considered voluptuous or sturdy, depending on one's relationship to it. Barbara Greenburg had gripped his arm and turned away with a moan. The dead woman's dress had been arranged primly over her knees, her hands clasped on her breast, and the man kneeling on the floor and against the bed placed an arm along the counterpane, so that the tableau resembled one of those ancient sepulchres that depicted in chiseled marble the immortal grief of a prince for his dead mistress. A small-caliber pistol was on the floor by the man's knee.

"Rose Donato?" Ryan asked. Then again, "Miss Greenburg, Rose Donato?"

"Yes, yes," Spearbroke's associate replied, shakily. He felt a little dizzy himself and looked toward the tall detective whose face was flushed; the man seemed angry about something. He stepped around the bed and leaned over the other corpse.

"I never met the gentleman," he nearly whispered.

"Perhaps, Mr. Spearbroke, you can give us a positive."

The literary agent nodded. He felt a numbness rising in his legs. "It's D. A. Prescott, Junior."

* * * * *

It was as if a wind swept over them, a terrible gale force that presaged a disaster, rather like looking up to see the large square radiator of the truck that pushes a wall of air before its determined course, and it was not until they stood in the calm, warming sunlight outside the apartment building that they felt safe. Barbara Greenburg had slipped on a pair of oversize sunglasses that ordinarily would have given her an attractive chic, but now only seemed to draw attention to the tenseness around her mouth. She shivered in the sun and her hands chafed her bare arms. Spearbroke took her hand and the two leaned against the edge of the sandstone balustrade beside the building's steps. They resembled a pair who awaited the departure of a train that would take only one of them to a destination far away.

It was with a mixture of relief and release, then, that they turned to Francis Ryan when he came out, as if his arrival on the scene had been the announcement for which the couple had been waiting to send them together on their way. He carried a squarish package and had paused to talk to them when a blue and white squad car from the Twentieth Precinct pulled up and stopped behind the rental sedan Kraft had left double-parked. Two uniformed police and a plain clothes detective got out, and Ryan held a brief conference with them at the curb. Then, leaving one of the cops at the door, the other two passed by Spearbroke and Greenburg and went up the stairs into the building. The plain clothes cop smiled pleasantly and wished them a good morning.

"I bet this is it," Ryan said as he returned. He held up the package. It was wrapped in brown paper, sealed, and with canceled postage. "Here's the exposé of the Lindsay administration." He held it out so that Spearbroke and Greenburg could read the mailing sticker. "You see, it's addressed to Adam McKendrick," the detective pointed out, "but that's the same box number in the Chelsea post office that West used for his airline tickets and bond sales."

"So what does that mean?" Spearbroke asked. "Hardy and McKendrick shared a postal box for their coauthorship? Or maybe," he turned to the young woman, "it was McKendrick's postal box and Hardy used it for his own purposes."

"I don't know what it means," Ryan almost spoke to himself as he continued to look at the label. He lifted the package in his hands as if its weight would reveal its contents, and a speculative mote formed in his clear blue eyes. "May I ask you a favor?"

"Yes, of course," Spearbroke said.

"If this is the manuscript, it wouldn't take long for the three of us to read it. If there is something in here," he raised the package, "we should be able to find it before more bodies appear."

"Something just occurred to me," Barbara Greenburg said as they walked to the sedan. "This package has never been opened. McKendrick apparently didn't care to see what Stratton had to say about his book. Does that sound like a writer's reaction to you?" She looked back at Spearbroke as she got into the backseat of the sedan. "I mean some of them even memorize their rejection slips."

"That's right," Spearbroke agreed. "Why was it so

unimportant to him?" he asked the detective, who had slipped into the front seat. Ryan looked amused by the question.

"I suspect it was unimportant to him," the policeman said softly, "because he never knew about it." He worked the blade of a small penknife around the edge of the sealed box. "I have a hunch that Adam McKendrick never wrote an exposé of anything, so the question is why it didn't matter to Hardy West when the manuscript was returned." He had sliced through the four sides of the package. "And if it were so unimportant to him, why do we have two bodies upstairs—why have three people been killed over a manuscript that is presumably so unimportant?"

" 'Dear Mr. McKendrick,' "

the detective read the letter.

> " 'We greatly appreciate the opportunity to read your manuscript The Lindsay Administration but I am sorry to say it does not suit our particular needs at the moment. I do wish you success with it and am sure it will find a suitable publisher.
>
> Sincerely,
> Dexter Corey.' "

"Form number three-twelve-dash-A," Greenburg said with a shrug. "What's the name of this opus again?"

"*The Lindsay Administration.*" Ryan referred to the boxed manuscript.

"There's a snappy title for you. A real grabber. Well, let's get to it. You know, I ought to get something extra for working on weekends."

Spearbroke ignored her remark and took the portion of manuscript that the detective had handed over the front seat. There were about three hundred pages in all, and they divided it equally among themselves. The car became quiet as the three read and turned the neatly typed pages. Barbara Greenburg had curled up in her corner of the rear seat, and Spearbroke stretched out his legs and leaned against the rear window. Francis Ryan crouched over the section that he had placed on the front cushion. Sunlight warmed the scents of new fabric and plastic in the car's interior. In a nearby building a radio blared a series of bulletins of traffic conditions on the city's bridges and tunnels. The volume was lowered abruptly, as if the unknown listener felt guilty to be listening to such a program. An elderly lady walked a Great Dane. The huge dog began to haul and pull on his leash, straining to a point on the street familiar only to him and right beside the car where the manuscript was being read. The dog assumed the tripodal position and casually licked its chops. The old lady dutifully observed her pet's elimination, complimented the animal on its success, and then led the dog back to the sidewalk to resume their walk, after she had scooped up his deposit.

Barbara Greenburg was becoming restless. Pages of the manuscript fanned loosely in her hands and she had begun to whistle under her breath, a signal Spearbroke recognized from working with her. She was bored and he knew the reason for it as he shuffled pages of the manuscript section in his hands. "Be patient," he soothed her. "I'm bored, too."

"What dreck," she drawled. "He had to be kidding."

"Just read for the scandal, whatever it was," the agent urged her and returned to his own copy. The detective seemed to be reading through the manuscript with the steady rhythm of a long-distance swimmer, page after page turned over with a lick of the thumb and forefinger. In fact, it was Ryan who finished his part of the chore first, silently collating the loose pages and looking through the windshield at the traffic on Amsterdam Avenue.

"You're done?" Spearbroke asked, amazed. He still had about twenty pages to go.

"I took a speed-reading course at Hunter College, night school," the policeman explained and then added, as if by way of an apology, "we have so many forms to go over, you know?"

"Shut up, will ya," muttered Barbara Greenburg. "It's hard enough to concentrate on this crap." The car became silent again. Two boys walked along the opposite sidewalk, in the direction of the park, as they tossed a soccer ball back and forth between them. Spearbroke read the last sentence with a deep breath. He looked at Barbara Greenburg. She seemed to have retreated, been made smaller by the task and, to pass the time, he reviewed in his mind the meticulous details of her petite person. His reverie became languorous. They had had only about two hours' sleep between them, and the warm spring sunlight laved this fatigue with a peculiar sense of well-being that was also slightly erotic. As if she had heard this buzz in his senses, Barbara Greenburg looked away from the manuscript and lifted the large buglike sunglasses to meet his reflection frankly, her eyes calm and receptive. The wide, heavy-lipped mouth smiled and then twisted down and to one side in an expression that carried many messages, all of them agreeable, all with humor.

She was the first to speak, after she had finished her part of the manuscript. "So what was exposed?"

"I found nothing." Spearbroke nodded.

"Nor I," Ryan agreed. "There's nothing here that I hadn't read in the newspapers at the time."

"That's it, too." Greenburg unlocked her legs and leaned forward, a little too far, Spearbroke thought, for he saw the policeman's eyes go to the front of her tank shirt. "A lot of this sounds like old newspaper stories. The style, you know. What do you think, Boss?"

Spearbroke nodded. "Yes, I caught that. Not consistent, but a mixture of journalistic styles. Not much coherence in mine, nothing really to hold it together." Ryan agreed, nodding.

"Me neither." Barbara Greenburg looked discomforted and handed her portion of manuscript to Ryan. "We've been had; someone's been had. No one could take this seriously. No wonder Buster Brown at Stratton reacted the way he did. I'd be insulted, too, if someone sent this to me."

Ryan put the manuscript back in order and into its box and fit the cover. "But say there had been a genuine exposé here, something that would connect these bodies. What would it be?"

"Well, it would have to be about politics. That's the subject here." Greenburg spoke quickly. Spearbroke was taken by her vibrancy, the intelligence in her face. "So, politics. What do we have?" she reasoned aloud, as if playing a parlor game. "Politics as the connection . . . well, how about old Prescott, the senator . . . anything about him? Don't all politicians have something to hide? But he's not mentioned at all in this manuscript, at least not in my part." The two men signaled similar findings.

"Let's continue, Ms. Greenburg." Detective Ryan turned to face her with an animated expression, a note of appreciation that made Spearbroke feel slightly uncomfortable. "Let's say there was some scandal about the late senator from New York. Who might know about it besides his accountant, lawyer, and priest?"

"His family," the young woman sighed.

"Or members thereof," the detective responded. "Put this together then with the large sums of money transferred to Hardy West, the airline reservations to South America." The man paused, a twinkle passing through his blue eyes.

"Aha." Greenburg sat forward on the edge of the car seat. "So Hardy West said to the Prescott family, here's this manuscript that has the goods on the old senator, so how about some getaway bucks and I'll keep it cool."

"Now just a minute," Spearbroke interrupted, quickly angry and just as quickly caught by the realization that he had easily accepted his friend as a murderer; but to have him accused of blackmail was somehow too much.

"You just-a-minute." She smiled. He could see his double reflection in her dark glasses. "You been had, Boss. We've all been had by Hardy West." He knew what she said was true, but he did not yet want to accept it.

Detective Kraft emerged from the apartment building and walked toward them, making a small detour around something beside the car. He leaned in the window on the driver's side. "The ME is on his way. The people in Westchester are going to notify the Prescott family and Mrs. West. The Twentieth guys are taking over here and I got warrants out for West. All routes are covered—airports and the like." Ryan nodded his approval. "This guy has been busy."

"I don't believe it," Spearbroke spoke up. "It's not in Hardy West to be a killer. He's a nice, soft, ineffectual . . ."

". . . mediocre writer," Barbara Greenburg finished for him.

"Yes." Spearbroke took a deep breath and somehow felt better for it. "A mediocre writer."

"Well, we want him for three murders," Ryan said. "That arrangement upstairs is about as poorly constructed as that exposé he wrote. Nobody kills and commits suicide like that." He motioned to his partner, who got into the car and turned on the engine. "What really makes me mad," the detective's voice seemed to be pulled thin and taut, "is the sacrilegious way that young woman was defaced."

It was an odd word to use for Gloria Benson's murder, but both people in the backseat solemnly agreed to its correctness. "Bastard," Barbara Greenburg muttered, and looked away from Spearbroke. He had to agree with her judgment.

"Shall we take you back to your place?" Kraft asked after a bit. The motor was idling smoothly.

"I want to talk with Gloria's parents when they get here," Barbara Greenburg reminded them.

"We can arrange that." Detective Ryan nodded as his partner put the car in gear.

"And I'll tell you what I want," Spearbroke said, then turned to Greenburg. "You drive, have a license, don't you?" She nodded. "Then I want to rent a car for the afternoon," he told the policeman.

"We can arrange that, too," Detective Kraft replied, and pulled at his long, sharp nose.

twelve

As they drove to Chappaqua, became part of the smooth belt of traffic that ran north from the city on Route 22, Spearbroke let his mind flow, surrendered control of his thoughts to let them take what form and go in which line they might. But whether connected or not, they all came together to circle around one fact that became the hub of his consciousness—it was only a week ago that he had met Hardy West for lunch and this bizarre and tragic set of circumstances had been started in motion.

And it had been a week, too, of changing relationships, the most important one being the one he shared with the young woman who maneuvered the car expertly from lane to lane through the late afternoon jam. Barbara Greenburg perched on the edge of the seat, her legs seemingly just long enough to reach the pedals on the floor, and gripped the steering wheel in both hands with an intensity that suggested some gymnastic discipline, as if she had only just managed to chin herself upon it.

"Look at that turkey," she said as another car pulled in front of her path. The driver had given no signal. She had changed from the sporty ensemble of the morning, actually the clothes in the small bag she had carried to Yoga camp, into a jacket and skirt of light tan with a tailored blouse in olive green, and as Spearbroke admired the details of her dress—the simple jewelry, the aroma of Madame Rochas that was just enough, the sandal straps that apportioned her small feet into neat sections—that made him appreciate the whole even more; as he admired all this in her he also gave some moment to the melancholy thought that their relationship had forever changed and, paradoxically, he found that the old camaraderie they had shared as business partners, the easygoing flirtations they had passed back and forth, these things he was more sorry to see disappear into the past than he was happy to greet the new and future relationship which, ironically, those flirtations had promoted.

"It seems to me," her rather harsh voice cut across his thoughts, "that this trip is above and beyond the normal client relationship." He said nothing and looked out the window. "You're going out here to comfort Libby West on the fact that her husband is a homicidal maniac."

"I still don't believe Hardy killed those people," he replied. "Yes, he might have tried that blackmail business, but not murder. No."

She bent over the wheel. She still wore the large-paned dark glasses and these had slipped down her nose. She set them right with a finger. "But I don't understand Prescott getting into it—to locate the manuscript, the family secret?"

"He was in it from the beginning. I would bet," Spearbroke speculated. "I'm pretty sure he pretended to be McKendrick on the phone. There was always something that bothered me about that conversation and I've finally remembered what it was. We started talking about the old days, the White Horse Tavern and all that. He didn't know the owner's correct name. He said it was Andy when everyone knew it was Ernie."

"Not everyone," Barbara Greenburg reminded him.

He turned and stared. "What was that?" His mind was racing.

She repeated, "Not everyone knew Andy/Ernie."

"Right. Well, I mean—Hardy West would have known the man's name. That's what I mean. Hardy West would have known and McKendrick would have known, but not D. A. Prescott, Junior. So when he called me from that pay phone outside McKendrick's apartment, I would bet he had found Adam's body, already killed, and he had probably taken the opportunity to search the apartment for the supposedly damaging manuscript."

"Would Libby West have known the man's name?" Spearbroke didn't answer, suddenly did not want to answer. He observed the suburban developments they passed. Barbara Greenburg continued. "So it was Junior Prescott who ransacked our office?"

"No doubt."

"What in hell do you suppose the old senator was up to that his son was so desperate to keep quiet?"

"Probably nothing much if put on the scale of current deceits," Spearbroke said as he fit a cigarette into his holder. He opened the ashtray compartment on the dashboard. It was packed with old cigarette butts and chewing gum wrappers, and the lighter did not work. "But something you must know, Greenburg, is that these old ruling families, this Eastern Seaboard nobility, put family honor on a pedestal and even the slightest jar is regarded as a serious threat."

"I suppose I must learn that if I'm going to be accepted. Here . . ." She pulled a book of matches from her suit pocket. "And Libby West? What of her?"

Spearbroke blew a stream of smoke out the open window. "Yes, what of her?" He saw her in his apartment last Sunday. The girl's laugh chased his reflection. "What?"

"You sound so . . . you sound hurt," she answered, one hand off the wheel as if to reach for the right word. "Say," she paused for another short catch of laughter, "how well do you know Libby West?"

"I hardly know her at all," he replied truthfully. "Hardly at all." They continued in silence for several minutes.

"Listen, Boss," Barbara Greenburg commenced speaking abruptly, as if sounding part of a phrase that played within her thoughts, "I've been thinking. One of the reasons I went to Long Island was to think about this, but I had an offer a while back from MCA to come over to take over their juvenile list and I think I'm going to do it." She had spoken the last dozen words in a rush as though she were afraid they might not pass her lips. Spearbroke was shocked.

"Well, you see," she continued in what he called her wise-guy routine, a mixture of New York street inflection and old gangster movies, "you got no kind of a retirement program in your firm. And there's no possibility of advancement, like upward mobility. You see?"

"I see." Spearbroke nodded slowly. "I'm sorry."

"You're always sorry. You're always apologizing. What is it with you WASPs?" She turned quickly to the rear to the traffic, and then swung into the right lane. "Can't you ever just enjoy something without apologizing, without feeling guilty?"

"You don't have to go."

"I know that, but listen—Ned." It was the first time he could remember her using his name and it made her sound more mature, more like his contemporary—a maturity he realized had been there all along. "There is a good reason," she had continued to say, "for that silly rule of yours. You know. I hate to admit it, but you're right. But don't get me wrong. I'm not sorry about anything. And don't you be. This is a super job over at MCA and I can go anywhere with it."

"I'm sure of it," he answered. There was no doubt it was true. Spearbroke breathed deeply and flipped his cigarette out the window. "Dear Barbara. Dear Greenburg."

"There you go again." Her voice sharpened. "You sound like Densher."

"Densher? Who's he?"

"Densher." She repeated the name with an emphatic gesture of her right hand, as if she were setting the letters out in midair. "Densher. James. Henry James." The proper names were almost printed rather than spoken. "Oh, you know." Now she seemed lost. "About the American girl who's dying . . . uh, what's-her-name . . . yes, Milly."

"Oh." Spearbroke brightened suddenly. *"Wings of the Dove."*

"Right." Barbara Greenburg nodded and then, not quite under her breath, "He's a great lay, but *t-h-i-c-k*. Here's the turn-off," she said, her speech shifting to a more normal level as the car passed a large highway sign with *Chappaqua* blazoned upon it.

Spearbroke remembered the route from his visit several days before, and directed her along the narrow, winding roads that seemed to be tunneled through the heavy green walls of privet and rhododendron that protected the estates on either side. There was a car parked at the entrance to the Prescott compound, a car so plainly black that it could just as easily have had the word POLICE painted in large letters across its hood, and the plainclothesman behind the wheel made no attempt to mask his scrutiny of them, their car, or its license plate.

Barbara Greenburg pulled their rental automobile

into position and parked beside a small green Mercedes convertible. It was very quiet and there was no sound from the converted gate house. He led the way around to the kitchen garden, the only entrance to the place he knew, and they stopped at the Dutch door, the bottom half closed. There was a stillness from within the house that was of a density to convince them that no one was at home. It was then, listening so intently for sounds inside the house, that they heard the curious sound behind them on the estate's grounds. It sounded like the soft chopping sounds of an ax, timed and steady. *Thwack—thwack—thwack.*

They followed the sounds down the gravel path between the privet hedges and to the tennis court. Libby West, properly attired in tennis costume, a blue bandana fastened close around her hair, stood at the baseline of the far court with a large wire basket of tennis balls beside her. White and yellow balls, like pearls from broken necklaces, were strewn on the ground of the opposite court. Slowly, her wiry body bent back, the ball was thrown high but exactly, and the racquet came up and over her head. *Thwack!* A perfect serve. Again, *thwack*. And then once more, *thwack*. She bent over the basket and took more balls from it.

Spearbroke felt awkward and wrongly dressed, as he had a few evenings before when he had come upon her and her brother playing their match. He walked down the short flight of steps to the court level—Greenburg had chosen to stay above—and then once standing on the clay surface of the court, he was unsure what he should do next. He was aware of the hard leather of his shoe's heels, nor was his indecision raised by Libby West. She continued to hit serves with near machinelike precision, standing only about twenty feet from Spearbroke, and with a fierce concentration that seemed to bring all the tendons and ligaments in her arms, neck, and legs to the surface of the skin, a delineation that was at once ugly and strangely beautiful and reminded Spearbroke, unhappily reminded him, of the passionate contortions of her body a week ago in his apartment. The only sign that she recognized her visitors, a slight flicker in the eyes, broke her concentration briefly, though it was just as quickly restored. A service ball bounced twice more before being placed high in midair before her head. *Thwack!*

So Spearbroke stood silently on the sidelines as she obviously intended him to do, to wait the moment when it would suit her to release him from his suspension in time and netted, as it were, by each of the hard, flat trajectories of her service. He admired her skill, her concentration. The balls skimmed over the net, only inches to spare, to strike the corners, the back line of the service area. She rarely faulted, and Spearbroke could not remember her serving this strongly or as accurately in the game with her brother. *Thwack!* It was the last ball from the wire basket, which she picked up by its handle to retrieve the supply.

"Good of you to come," she said without looking at him. Her voice seemed strained, as if the neck muscles had pressed too tight. It was only then, as she passed him on her way to the far court, that he noticed her face bore traces of tears as well as sweat. He followed her, trying to tread as lightly as possible.

"I don't suppose you've heard from Hardy?" he asked.

"Not likely," she answered over her shoulder. Briskly, she went about picking up the spent tennis balls—the basket had a hinged panel in its bottom that trapped them when it was lowered over them—and he once again found himself barred from approaching her by the court's lines, as a person who cannot swim must stand on the shore and witness someone helpless in the sea.

"I've told all I know to the cops," she said. "He was blackmailing me—us. He had got together with this McKendrick and was using information that he knew, that I told him." She paused in her task. "I told him the night we were married . . . that my father, the respected senator, abused me when I was a child." She had placed the tennis racquet across her breast and then, in sudden anger, a fury no less extreme for the sudden softening of her face, dropped a ball she had just picked up and hit it with such force that it struck the steel mesh of the enclosure's fence and wedged there, almost passed through. "Goddamned son of a bitch," she said throatily.

"But, Libby." Spearbroke raised his arms. "There was nothing. There was nothing in the manuscript. I've read it." She had stopped and looked blankly toward him. Her eyebrows had been so bleached that they were almost invisible. "There was nothing in that manuscript," he repeated, "but a collation of old newspaper and magazine stories about the Lindsay administration. It was a farce, a hoax."

She had resumed retrieving the tennis balls, several dozen in all. "But, why, then, did Hardy kill this McKendrick?"

"But Hardy didn't kill McKendrick! The man's murder was just a coincidence, an urban accident. They've caught the juvenile who mugged him." It was then, as if Barbara Greenburg had only come on the scene, that Libby West noticed her, looked up at her. It was a sudden reaction, as if Spearbroke's associate had uttered a profanity or performed some outlandish gesture. Libby turned her back, shaking her head.

"We thought he had," she said. "We thought he had murdered McKendrick to keep him quiet. After we paid Hardy off, we figured that McKendrick had threatened to tell what he knew . . ."

"He knew nothing," Spearbroke said quietly. "He didn't even know about any manuscript. Hardy was only using his name."

". . . so Junior," she had paused only long enough to comprehend this last bit of information, "Junior thought . . . Junior thought this would be a good opportunity to get rid of Hardy. I tried everything to talk him out of it. Let him go, I pleaded. But Junior ran things his way always. There was no way I could stop him. But you see, Hardy knew and he had challenged Junior too many times, made fun of him too many times and Junior was . . ." her voice faltered, then resumed, "Junior was no one to play games with if you didn't play by the rules. His rules," she added. Then she waved her racquet toward Barbara Greenburg. "Then, Miss Kinky wrote you that card."

"You have her all wrong. It's all a lot of talk. She's not that way at all," Spearbroke defended his associate.

"I see," Libby West said as she studied her racquet's head. "Since last Sunday, you've learned she is different."

"Ah," Spearbroke sighed, and glanced toward Greenburg, who stood quietly, seeming not to have heard their talk, but watchful.

"Junior thought . . . we thought that your assistant had heard it, too, had heard something, so as not to take a chance, he decided . . . we decided to . . . to . . ." She could not finish, and only wagged the racquet before her.

His breath was short, his voice tight, and the words hurt his throat. "And it was supposed to appear as if she had been accidentally killed while submitting to one of her supposed sexual fantasies. Which you had heard about that Sunday with me." She nodded and retrieved the last of the balls. "And you also got her address somehow that Sunday." She nodded once more.

"But you see we still hadn't found the manuscript." Her expression was clean, the eyes sparkled with the innocent pique of a child. Spearbroke felt revulsion. He felt betrayed, lured by the manicured and privileged manner of her person, as he now stood on the strange surface of this tennis court; lured by these very qualities of class and prestige, only to discover they made for a very thin lawn poised over a bottomless pool of filth.

"What in hell was so terrible about this family secret," his voice had become thin with anger and disgust, "that people had to be killed?" She had returned to her practice, served another ball. "Was it some political scandal? Something about your father?" He walked around the baseline and put out a hand to stop the racquet. "Libby?"

Barbara Greenburg had been observing this interview from the terrace, most of the conversation on the court rising to her hearing on the soft, warm gusts of the fine weather, though some of it was drowned in the sporadic outbursts of robins and bluejays. But she had heard enough, and she turned away.

Ned Spearbroke looked different to her, or, perhaps, she looked differently at him—his shoulders were really quite broad—and she had been enjoying watching him as he pursued and confronted Libby West. She promised herself other such studies, even as he did commonplace things, and she felt like a student trying to make up a subject too long ignored. But the lithe tennis player's answer had made her turn away, an involuntary gesture she wished Ned Spearbroke would imitate for the sake of their newfound innocence.

"I asked you out here that night . . . ," Libby

turned to look at him. "I'm sorry, Ned, about that evening . . . so that Junior could get into your place and look for it. It hadn't been at McKendrick's, it hadn't been at the other apartment, and when he couldn't find it in your office—he went wild. There was a connection, we figured, with whoever your associate had met at her Yoga camp."

"So how did you find Rose Donato's address? You know, incidentally, she was trying to get rid of Hardy, had no intention of going away with him." The information did not seem to surprise her. Or perhaps, he thought, it did not matter to her.

"It was simple. Junior called the camp pretending to be Barbara Greenburg's brother, saying she had misplaced something, a watch, and asked for the names and addresses of those she shared sleeping quarters with. The girl from Ohio was clearly not the one."

"Iowa."

"What?" Libby West looked at him critically. She had regained her composure by now.

"She was from Iowa, the girl in Barbara's apartment."

"Well, one of those places." Libby bounced a ball. "But the other one sounded familiar. I had a notion of this tutti-frutti anyway—Hardy was rather childish in letting me know about his little heats—and the name Rose had been dropped a few times. It's not a name one hears very often."

"Jesus Christ." Spearbroke sighed, and he felt ashamed. She shrugged her shoulders. He looked at Barbara Greenburg on the terrace. He took a deep breath, turned his back on Libby West, and began to talk in the direction of the half-log steps. *Thwack!* She had begun to serve once more.

"But you know what this has done for me?" she

said almost giddily. "I'm free of all them." *Thwack!* "Every goddamn one of them—Hardy—Daddy—Junior—" *Thwack!* "No more done for, did to." *Thwack.* "I've got my own game, now. I run everything now." She seemed to take special aim at the far court, pulled her lithe figure into a taut bow that sprung to loose the ball with great velocity.

They could still hear the regular explosions of her service as they got into the car. "You heard everything?" Spearbroke asked Barbara Greenburg. She nodded and looked at him and he saw her petite figure come together, her face clench almost, and, though only a recent authority on these dear assemblies, he recognized that his assistant was making a great effort to stay calm. Then, out of the corner of her mouth, she said. "My people have a saying: 'Once the loaf has been cut, what does another slice matter?' "

"Quite so," Spearbroke replied. As they drove out of the estate, the well-tended stillness around them was clipped by the chop-chop service of the solitary tennis player.

thirteen

Sunday nights were always quiet at Irene's. The tourists had returned to their suburban roots and the fashionable coop on the Upper East Side was given back to the regulars. Irene stood at the end of the bar, totaling up the evening's receipts, a small computer at her right hand. A spirited game of backgammon was in progress at a rear table, and a crowd from the *Paris Review* argued at a table near the one where Spearbroke and Barbara Greenburg sat holding hands.

There was a chill in the evening, one of those last gusts of spring that will sweep the city before the heavy breath of summer smothers all, and the young woman wore an oversize sweater, jeans, and sneakers. Spearbroke was dressed similarly, and they resembled a hungry couple who had just left their bed and who, in their hurry for food, had somehow mixed up some of their clothes. And, indeed, this is what had happened.

"It's a small town," she was saying to him. "We'll see each other."

"But it won't be the same."

"It can't be the same." She shook her head. "You want too many things. Business associates. Comrades." She threw back her head in a dramatic fashion. "Lovers. Listen, I'll tell you what, I'll come over on Sundays and we can do naughty things with the *Times* crossword puzzle."

"It sounds homey," he said dryly, and lit a cigarette. "See that couple over there?" He directed her attention to a corner table where the aging juvenile star of a Walt Disney series sat across from a very pretty young woman. At first glance, the couple seemed to be about the same age, but a second look revealed the great difference between them, not so much the superficial physical disparities—the man's face had relatively few wrinkles—but in the contrast of their behavior. The girl talked with great animation, employing all of her fingers to make several points at once, it would seem, while her companion reacted slowly, smiled slowly, and moved his head this way or that with an evenness that implied experience and wisdom or perhaps, Spearbroke thought, a wise caution not to unnecessarily ripple his surface. "What would you say is their relationship?" he asked.

"Oh, I get it." Greenburg's voice climbed into the upper parts of her head. He would miss that harsh sound. "I'd say they're both making it in their different ways."

"Yes, making it," Spearbroke said after a long drag on the ebony cigarette holder. "That's the term. But I'm more interested in starting out. It has more diversity, I think. I would bet she lives in a cold-water flat . . ."

". . . and suffers from incipient TB," Greenburg said, picking up her glass of white wine. "You're hopeless," she added.

"But I'm not being romantic," he insisted. The entrance door swung creakily and everything seemed to pause in the restaurant. A man in a raincoat stood for a moment, then walked to the bar. "I'm not," he continued. "I think of all the cold-water flats, all the bookcases made of planks of wood and bricks, and all the one-hundred-and-one ways to fix noodles and tuna fish—there are some of us, like Hardy West, who never get beyond that stage, who are forever starting out, fixing up a place in which to make it, but never quite getting it fixed up."

"Yeah, so? But you're suggesting some idealistic alliance is being worked out over there." She inclined her head toward the corner table. "That old Skippy Trueheart is sharing his wisdom with Miss Goody as an act of paternal beneficence and that from that I'm to draw some paradigmatical inference about our relationship. But let me set you straight, Spear-love, you don't have to screw us to save us. Nor does it work the other way. Screwing is fine and salvation is okay, too, but they are not related." She dipped a piece of hard roll into her wine and sucked it.

"Ah, Greenburg," the agent breathed, "surely I have much to learn from you." It amused him that in the short course of the last couple of days, her manner of address had undergone so many changes, from the rather formal *Boss* to the spontaneous variation she had just employed—and not to mention the different things she had called him in bed; one more example, if one were needed, of how a person can be characterized, if not created, by a given nomenclature. It was just then that Hardy West stepped into the restaurant.

The writer looked weary. He was unshaven and red-eyed. His clothes hung on him like stolen laundry and he paused at the entrance to look around, as if to see if he would be recognized. Irene had left her post by the computer and came toward him, her heavy arms out to enfold and draw his handsome head down to her broad bosom. It was an honor she reserved for her most famous customers.

"Do you want something to eat?" She mothered him when they got to Spearbroke's table. West shook his head, though his eyes had not left his agent's face.

Spearbroke's expression was a mixture of disbelief and anger.

"Maybe a drink," Hardy West said hoarsely. He pushed a hand through the heavy bronzed hair as he placed the blue box he had been carrying on the table near Barbara Greenburg. "Scotch and water."

"Right," Irene replied as her hand went above her head and a waiter was magically beside her.

The writer's fatigue and dishevelment seemed only to make him more attractive and, because he was certain of what he would see, Spearbroke checked the small table in the corner. Sure enough, the young woman's intense concentration on her matinee idol had been broken, and she stared at Hardy West with undisguised interest.

"I'm glad you could join us," Spearbroke said, fitting a new Gauloise into the black holder. "You've talked to but never met Miss Greenburg." Hardy West nodded solemnly and sat down, and she folded and leaned forward on her arms as if to forestall any attempt he might make to shake hands. The waiter brought West his drink and set it before him. Dice rattled in the backgammon cup behind them.

"I'm sorry," Hardy West said after taking a drink. He nodded. "I'm truly sorry."

"Yes, well, we're all sorry," Spearbroke said tightly, putting out his cigarette. "There's a family in Des Moines, Iowa, that's especially sorry. Also, Rose Donato's family is very sorry. Barbara Greenburg is sorry; we're all . . ."

"Poor Rose," West continued calmly, as if impervious to Spearbroke's scorn.

"That was all your stuff, the lumber and tools, in her apartment?" Spearbroke asked. "Always fixing up a place in which to write the Great American Novel."

"And I did . . . I have," West said, tapping the top of the blue box. "She had just finished typing it; I was going to send it to you after we left . . . I never dreamed she would disappear, that she didn't want to go away with me."

"Oh, boy." Barbara Greenburg sighed and raised her eyes to the ceiling.

"That's how you met McKendrick again?"

"I never met him. He answered one of Rose's ads in the *Village Voice.* He had become one of these letter-to-the-editor freaks and needed her to type them. Long, involved letters about pollution. The welfare system."

"So, it was your idea to put together this bogus manuscript about the Lindsay administration under McKendrick's name and to blackmail the Prescotts about what it supposedly contained?" As he spoke, the agent saw Detective Kraft walk slowly through the front door and up to the bar, where he ordered a beer and began to read a newspaper he took from his pocket. "I daresay, Hardy," Spearbroke continued, "the transition you had to make between John Lindsay's manipulation by the city unions and your wife's sexual abuse by her father, the late senator, must have been masterful. Something akin only to Somerset Maugham, I would imagine. I'd give anything to have seen it."

"Oh, come on, Ned—not Maugham. I know I've behaved badly, but I deserve better than that. But none of it was down on paper. You've seen the manuscript. I only told them I had written it down. All about her father and her. She didn't tell you about little brother, I guess. Oh, sure," West responded to Spearbroke's surprised grunt. "I came on the two of them once in the greenhouse. I remember I was looking for some lumber—I was building a cold frame for seedlings. I remember, and—"

"Yes, yes," Spearbroke interrupted. Hardy West's grasp of exposition had always been much too loose.

"Well, Libby is a woman of strong appetites," West continued. "But perhaps you know that."

If a man of fifty can look insolent—the expression mostly given to the young—Hardy West faced his agent with just such a mien, and Spearbroke felt his face warmed by the scrutiny. He dared not look at Barbara Greenburg, but he felt the keen, quick flicker of her eyes on him. He scrounged within himself to collect his breath and manner so that when he spoke he would sound like his old self. Though he knew that much had changed.

"So, the old bugaboo of incest . . ."

"The idea was to get away," West said quietly. "I would suppress the manuscript, all the supposed revelations included, and they would set me up somewhere so I could start fresh." He sipped his drink. "That was the plan. But then Junior killed McKendrick, and I figured he didn't trust me."

"How dense of him." Barbara Greenburg turned and crossed her legs.

"I became afraid he would try to kill me, too. Rose also, if he found her. But by then she had disappeared. The whole business was coming apart. I didn't know where she had gone, so I stayed here, hoping to protect her." He looked at Barbara Greenburg pleadingly, as if he hoped to win her to his side. "But, I was too late."

"D. A. Prescott, Junior, didn't kill McKendrick," Spearbroke told West. The information seemed to push the man against his chair. "He was mugged. Only mugged."

A chair scraped behind them and one of the players in the backgammon game stood up and came toward them. It was Detective Ryan, and he sat down in a chair beside West and spoke in a normal conversational tone, as if it were an ordinary subject they discussed.

"Mr. West, I'm Detective Francis Ryan," he showed an open billfold to the writer, "of the New York City Police Department, and this person," he signaled to their waiter who had just clipped a gold badge to his shirt pocket, "is Detective Madison of the Fifth Homicide." The policeman took a chair and sat on the other side of West. "My partner, as you see, is by the door. We have warrants for your arrest on the charges of murder of one Rose Donato, and D. A. Prescott, Junior, and for conspiracy to commit murder and for conspiracy to commit fraud. It is my responsibility to warn you of your Constitutional rights, that you are entitled to remain silent until you—"

"Yes, yes," Hardy West interrupted, a note of relief in his voice, "I waive all that."

Detective Ryan had gestured toward the corner table and the young woman left the motion picture star and came toward them. "This is Jane Crowell, whose address is one eighty-seven West Seventy-seventh Street, the same building lived in by Rose Donato." He had no further introductions, and Spearbroke suspended a move to rise to greet her. "Miss Crowell, do you recognize anyone here at this table, in addition to those police officers whom you have already met?"

"Yes, this gentleman. Mr. West."

"When and how have you seen him?"

"He came and went frequently from Rose . . . Miss Donato's apartment."

"And yesterday?"

"Yes, yesterday morning. I was coming back from the store . . ."

"About what time?"

"Around eight-thirty, nine o'clock and he came running down the stairs. Nearly knocked me down."

"I'm sorry about that," Hardy West said to her earnestly. "But I didn't kill Rose."

"Thank you," Ryan said, dismissing her. "We'll call you later, if it's necessary." She returned quickly to her table, as if she were now free to pursue a more important errand. She shook hands with the actor. He stood and helped her on with her raincoat and waved to her once more as she left. Then, carrying his highball glass, he walked to the rear of the restaurant.

"I came into the apartment—I had spent the night in Chinatown, a cheap place," West looked away, as if the modesty of the lodgings would excuse why he had had to make that choice. "Junior was tapping out that message on the typewriter as I came in and I took him by surprise. He tried to shoot me but we wrestled a bit and the gun went off. I . . . I panicked then and fixed him beside . . . Rose. He had already killed her. I guess he was going to wait for me."

He shook his head and the group became silent. Spearbroke regarded Barbara Greenburg, who in turn studied the worn profile of Hardy West.

"Irene would like to buy a round." One of the actual waiters had approached.

"Nothing for us," Francis Ryan said, a hand on West's arm. The others shook their heads. A speculative light caught in the detective's expression. "That about wraps it up, I guess, except for Mrs. West. She's clearly a part of this, an accessory, but we have no hard evidence, nothing to make the charge stick. She has the best lawyers, you know."

Spearbroke had studied the checkered tablecloth, counted the red and white squares of the design as if looking for an extraordinary move in a game he could not win but that he might prolong if he could find the strategy. He had almost felt the detective's eyes flick over him. He looked at Ryan. "Perhaps," he said after a deep breath, "I might be able to help you with that."

"Ah, that would be very good of you, Mr. Spearbroke," Francis Ryan replied smoothly, and put out his hand. "The morning will do fine. We'll be in touch."

Barbara Greenburg's large cat's eyes had become soft and luminous when Spearbroke eventually looked into them. She dipped a finger in her wine, made an X in the air with the moistened tip, and winked.

"You know, jail might not be so bad." It had been Hardy West who spoke, and the others at the table turned and regarded him as if he were a stranger who had just crashed their table, one of those tourists whom Irene always tried to discourage.

"What's that?" Spearbroke finally asked.

"I said, jail might not be so bad. You know, for me to get some work done." West had looked at Detective Ryan as if his words were meant more for his benefit than the others, as if they were to ease the policeman's duty.

"Peace and quiet, you mean," Spearbroke said sarcastically. "Someplace where you can do the Great American Novel, is that it?" He reached for the blue box on the table. "What is this supposed to be?" Ryan had also placed a hand on the manuscript, paused, and then released it to the agent.

"Wait until you read it," Hardy West said with an eagerness that appalled the agent.

"Yes," Spearbroke said tiredly, "yes, Hardy, I'll read it." The policmen grouped around the writer and walked him through the door and out into the night. Only a few in the restaurant noticed their exit.

"Well," Spearbroke said, "it's been quite a night." He fixed another cigarette into its holder. "Are you still hungry?" He smiled at his companion.

"Starved." Greenburg stretched her arms above her head. The loose sleeves of his sweater slipped down her slender arms. "I'm . . . I'm happy to know you, Boss."

"Your usage, Greenburg, makes for ambiguity." He took a deep drag on the strong tobacco. "On the other hand, perhaps it's possible to prove the authenticity of your happiness in my company." He chose his words carefully.

"So, okay." She grinned. "Can I get something to eat first? Or, do I have to read this manuscript? Or what? You tell me."

"You guys ready to order?" Irene had coasted over as if on very large ball bearings. "Oh, say, with all the excitement, I forgot to tell you. There was a guy in here earlier looking for you."

"Who was it?" Ned Spearbroke asked.

"I dunno," Irene shrugged. "Nobody I recognized."